On a Scale of One to Ten

A novel by

Sandi Underwood

-
- ON A SCALE OF ONE TO TEN Copyright ©2021
- Line By Lion Publications
- www.pixelandpen.studio
- ISBN: 978-1-948807-60-9
-
-
-
- Cover Art:Thomas Lamkin Jr.
- Editing By:Ian Jedlica
-

LINE BY LION
PUBLICATIONS

For Faith

For fun?

Chapter 1

Aliens Walk Among Us

My name is Amanda Jo Ketchings and I see dead people—oh, not what you're thinking; the dead people I see are spread out in coffins, dressed in their Sunday best with blankets of satin cradling their lifeless bodies, and flowers of all sizes and colors poking out from every available nook and cranny.

I live in a small town in Iowa above the only funeral home around, along with Mom and Dad—two of the dullest people on earth. We have zero in common, my parents and I, and even though I love them to death, no pun intended, let's face it, hip they are not.

My not-so-exciting home life, not-so-hip parents, and not-so-many friends probably explain why I am the least popular girl in school. That's not only my opinion—just ask the chosen ones, the cheerleaders, and the prom queens. On a scale of one to ten, my life sucks at a minus twelve.

However, there's always hope. After I finish this semester, I will say sayonara to Middle School and begin a new chapter in my, up-until-now, boring life. Yes, next year

I embark on the long-awaited journey down the sacred halls of Mill Oak High. Even stringing those words together sends chills down my spine.

My long-term goal as I shift toward my sophomore and junior years, and especially my illustrious senior year, is to face each day with one goal in mind—to move far, far away from this do-nothing town and my do-nothing life. Every year will bring me closer to my life-long dream of becoming a fashion designer in New York City where I will hop from one subway to the next and hang out at trendy little bars that have names like Tofu & You or Je'taime Escargot. Actually, the thought of snails makes me hurl, but the name just sounds cool, and cool is what I plan for my life to be—cool Amanda Jo Ketchings.

"Amanda Jo Ketchings!"

I jumped a foot as Mom's voice pierced the air like a jagged lightning bolt.

"Clean your room. We're having company for dinner."

Jerking back to reality, I didn't even attempt to mask my smirk. "So, they won't eat in my room, right?" I might be plain Jane with my frizzy hair and thunder thighs, but my sense of humor cracks me up; besides, if I didn't laugh, I'd cry—that's how bad my life sucks.

"Amanda Jo, clean your room right now!" Mom's proclamation measured a 0.4 on the Richter scale.

Hurling my feet off the bed, I snagged one toe in a denim jacket and awarded it a hefty lob toward the closet, but one sleeve caught on a ceiling fan blade and carouselled around and around like a headless ghost on a carnival ride. *Now that's pretty funny.*

Mom's head ducked back around my door, before calling out, "And wear your new dress." She continued down the hall, but not before flinging one last exhortation. "I said *CLEAN YOUR ROOM!*"

"Wah-wah-wah." I mimicked under my breath while straightening a stack of TEEN SCENE magazines into a neat pile. "So, who's coming to dinner that's so life-and-death?" My voice rattled down the hallway.

"A family your dad met at the conference in New York."

One brow shot up. *New York...did she say New York?* I vaulted from my bed and attacked the stack of books and papers strewn on the floor before opening a dresser drawer and swiping the contents from its cluttered top onto the half-folded undies stored inside. With a couple of hefty kicks, my shoes and socks cannonballed under the bed while I stacked throw pillows into a line like I'd seen on TV before raking a quick hand over the wrinkled topper. *Not bad—not good—but better.*

I shimmied into the mint green dress while scooting my bare feet into black ballet slippers and applied a couple of licks with a hairbrush. When our guest arrived a half-hour later, I was totally star-struck.

Chapter 1

Surprise!

Ambriel Chambers, the most elegant lady I'd seen, like ever, floated inside the door before turning back to indicate the two people standing behind her. She parted her perfectly outlined lips and liquid silk oozed out.

First, she introduced a skinny girl with long, limp hair. "This is my daughter, Elle," and turning to Dad, she purred, "and you already know my husband, Jay."

Tearing my gaze from the beautiful lady, my eyes leaped to the stick figure, Elle. Beautiful name, but this Elle was anything *but* beautiful–matter of fact, standing beside her, *I* could almost pass for beautiful, and that's a stretch.

Elle's thick eyebrows framed a hollow face that ended with a sharp pointy chin, and her nose had a hump in the middle that would make an eagle sit up and pay attention. Mousey-brown hair hung like over-cooked noodles on either side of ears last seen on a jack-rabbit. Talk about un-beautiful, this girl lived in a whole 'nother zip code.

My eyes skip-hopped back to Mrs. Chambers with her flawless face and delicately-arched brows cradled by shiny blonde hair that flipped out ever-so-slightly screaming *I'm too sexy for my head*. I was 100 percent captivated.

To say Elle didn't get her looks from her mother is an understatement.

I jerked my head around to study Jay. Think ex-football player turned ESPN anchorman, complete with a few gray streaks decorating his temples, and his lean frame sporting expensive-looking duds, boasting a swagger that bragged about games won, both on and off, the field.

No family resemblance there, either. Elle must be adopted.

"Won't you come in?" Mom asked.

It was precisely that moment I realized my mouth hung open like the trap door to our attic. I snapped it shut and shadowed them into the living room.

Mom placed a firm hand on my back and maneuvered me toward the stairs. "Amanda Jo, why don't you show Elle your room? I'll call you when dinner is ready."

"Sure." My look didn't make it to the other girl's eyes. "Follow me, Elle."

Elle followed without a peep.

Halfway down the hall, I turned. "You want to see *my* room or the embalming room?" This place has a few perks, and I was more than willing to cash in.

"I've seen my share of embalming rooms." Elle's unimpressed tone screamed 'been there, done that'.

"You have?" My plan of intimidation flew right out the proverbial window. "I forget it's there, but it's all my friends want to talk about." No need to share the fact I have zero friends or visitors of any kind, so instead, I flipped on the light in my room and closed the door behind us to drown out the grown-up voices. "So, what do you think of our hick town, and why are you here, anyway?"

"Town's okay," she said, "but we only arrived last night. We're over at Hillsboro Inn. Pool's nice."

"No way is this town a vacation destination, so why are you here?" I repeated the question.

She flashed big eyes at me. "I guess we are considering relocating here…I figured you knew that."

"Why would I know that?" I furrowed my eyebrows to better concentrate. Maybe I missed that conversation at the dinner table.

Elle marched over to my bed and plopped down puffing her limp hair momentarily before it surrendered back into humdrum. "Like I said, I figured you knew my dad is going into business with your dad."

Chapter 3

The Mask

"Wait, what???" I peered at the pretzel-thin person perched on my bed wearing a light blue Cashmere sweater that barely concealed the pointy peaks of each shoulder. *Is she anorexic?* "You're kidding, right? Your family intends to relocate here, in this boring, do-nothing town, from none other than New York City to be a partner in this tiny little funeral home, which has, what, six or seven funerals a month max? What am I missing?"

Elle's questioning gaze intersected mine before she quickly averted her eyes. "If you don't know, then maybe it's not a done deal." She tugged her skirt down over one knee, but not before I caught a glimpse of a gigantic bruise.

Rather than acknowledging what I saw, I focused on what I heard. "Hmmmm…Since when does Dad need a business partner? I've never heard that before."

Mom opened the door with one knock, her smile stretched ear to ear, and she appeared thrilled to see me. Like, that never happens. "Dinner, girls."

Seated around the dinner table, I soon realized Elle's mother was the talker of the family. Mrs. Chambers prattled on and on about her house in New York, Broadway shows, and the fabulous fashion district. Apparently, she was involved in every charity event this side of Canada. Why would she even think about, let alone agree to, moving to this boring town? Surely, I had misunderstood Elle.

"Now Amy," Mr. Chambers interrupted my thoughts with a voice rougher than sandpaper. "I'm sure these folks aren't interested in how you spend your day in New York City."

"I am." The words gushed out as the blood rushed to my face.

Mom's hand halted in mid-air as she passed the basket of rolls. "Amanda Jo has grand illusions about becoming a fashion designer and moving to New York City one day, although I tell her she needs to get her high school diploma first. Roll?"

Mr. Chambers accepted a roll as his laughter chimed in with the other chuckles around the table.

My shoulders sagged closer to my plate, and my face stung as if tiny bees stabbed every inch.

Mrs. Chambers looked me right in the eye and smiled before reaching over to pat my arm, which made me blush even more. "Why, I think that's a fine career, Amanda Jo. What kind of fashion are you interested in? Who are some of your favorite designers?"

Usually, I could rattle off all the top designers and even a few of the unknown ones, but with all this attention, my throat tightened, and my mind went blank. "All kinds, I guess."

"Well, maybe I can show you around one day." Mrs. Chambers volleyed a look toward her daughter. "Wouldn't it be fun if Elle and you could accompany me on a little outing to New York someday...that is if we move here?" She ripped her eyes from her daughter to her husband, and even though her smile didn't diminish, her previously dazzling blue eyes did.

So maybe they *are* moving here, and maybe the move was supposed to be a secret, and maybe Mrs. Chambers just spilled the beans. Whatever the reason behind her strange look, I liked her, but how could you *not* like someone so pretty and thoughtful? Then, realizing the full impact of what she just said, my head jerked up...it was true. They were moving to Iowa from New York City!

A flash of light from Elle's plate interrupted my roller-coaster thoughts as her right hand grasped her fork in a death-grip while she pushed food from one side of Mom's Noritake china plate to the other.

Mrs. Chambers' eyes fixed on her daughter. "Elle, eat your dinner, sweetie, so Mrs. Ketchings won't think you don't care for her cooking...now we don't want that, do we?"

Elle's pained face shot up. "Oh, Mrs. Ketchings, I'm just not very hungry...I promise everything tastes really good, but you see I had a Coke right before I left home, and it killed my appetite."

Her expression reminded me of a mask I'd seen hanging in a theater last year that was alabaster white with the mouth turned down at the corners. "Lots of killed appetites wind up here." I glanced around the room to see if anyone caught my joke, but the glare in Mom's eyes told me she hadn't.

Mr. Chambers and Dad left the table to watch ESPN in the living room, and Mrs. Chambers jumped up to help Mom clear the table, while I made a dash for my room with Elle following in that silent way of hers as if she wanted to fade into the wallpaper and disappear.

"Want to watch MTV?"

She stood in the doorway rubbing her arm as if it itched. "Mom won't allow me to watch that channel."

My gaze sprang to a huge red splotch covering the skin below her elbow. "Hey, wait–did you just hurt your arm? Did you run into something in the hall?"

Her face flushed beet-red. "No, I...it's nothing...probably just a mosquito bite or something."

I decided to drop it, but I couldn't help but wonder about that mark on Elle's arm. Did she run into the wall or was it self-inflicted? Surely my imagination was running rampant. "Well, *Mom's* not here and *Mom* won't know we watched MTV unless you tell her." Still, that red spot looked questionable.

She retraced her steps to the same corner of my bed and plopped down. "She'll quiz me later about what we did. She always does."

I clicked on the remote and turned down the volume. "So, tell her we just hung out…she doesn't have to know details, right?"

Her face bordered somewhere between the expression I make when I swallow Pepto Bismol and lemonade that needs more sugar. When she spoke, her voice was weak, and her eyes dull. "I am not allowed to lie to my parents."

Not lie to your parents–wasn't that almost a given? The trick was not to get caught. "You're kidding, right?" My eyebrows skated up my forehead. "You're serious! Look, we don't have to watch TV, we can check out FacePage, instead."

Elle didn't move a muscle while I signed onto the Internet.

I glanced at her once or twice, but she appeared to be glued to my bed, still rubbing that arm. "You ARE on FacePage, right?"

"No." She made the tiniest squeak possible that could still pass for a word.

There was something badly wrong with this girl, and I was just the person to learn the truth. "So, what *do* you do for fun?" I turned around to study her face, which had potential if she'd pull her hair back in a ponytail, smear on a little mascara, and add lip gloss.

"I have a lot of homework."

"Yeah, but what do you do for fun? Like, when your parents aren't around? I mean, I've never been to New York City, but from what I see on TV, they have EVERYTHING there." I clicked off the items on my fingers. "Ice skating in the winter right downtown, Macy's Thanksgiving Day Parade, Lion King showing on Broadway, shopping malls full of designer stores where my own designer fashions someday will be sold, Central Park, hot dog stands on street corners... and the big New Year's Eve party where the ball drops and the year changes. How fun is that?"

"I go shopping with Mom a lot and we meet her friends for lunch."

I scrunched my nose. "Yeah, that's what I'm talking about–spending time with Mom, right? How lame is that?" I grinned to let her know I was on to her, but she didn't flinch. *"You're kidding!"* My mouth dropped open again and I rolled my desk chair across the floor to prop my feet on the bed. There was a story here and I intended to uncover it. "So, do you have a boyfriend back in the Big Apple?"

"Nope." Her thin shoulders lifted and dropped.

"A best friend?"

"Nope."

"Cousins?"

Her gray eyes met mine. "No cousins. One aunt." She batted her eyes and stared out the window. "We move around a lot."

"What's that like–moving? We've never moved, lived right here in the same spot all my life, but when I graduate I'm moving to New York. Hey, maybe you can help me find a place to live." I shoved off the bed with one foot and rolled back to my laptop to see who'd pinged my FacePage. "No, wait." I looked back at Elle. "You'll be living here by then, right? How mixed up is that?"

Her eyes met mine. "I *hope* we do move here. I like it."

"You're kidding, right? It has to be Boresville compared to New York City. There's nothing going on around here, no fun, no exciting places to eat, no great places to shop, no subway to ride, and certainly no Broadway shows. Why would you ever want to move *here*?"

On a scale of one to ten, the look in Elle's eyes made me feel like one and a half.

"We always start over someplace else."

"But why?"

"Because." As if that explained everything.

I crossed one foot over the other. "I don't understand why you need to start over someplace else when your dad owns a funeral home in New York...I mean, New York, for crying out loud! People must die there every day."

"Not anymore."

"People no longer die in New York?"

"Of course, they do, it's just my dad no longer owns a funeral home there."

"So, he sold it?"

"I guess."

I gestured with my hands. "So, either he did sell it, or he didn't sell it...like, he owned one before, but he doesn't today?"

"Something like that." Her eyes darted around the room.

I shrugged my shoulders. "That doesn't make sense, but it's not any of my business." I decided to change the subject. "So, how'd you get that bruise on your knee?"

Elle placed her hand over her knee and rubbed it–kind of like she'd rubbed her elbow just moments ago. "I don't remember."

When she clasped her hands in her lap, I rolled closer to have a better look. "You got that big bruise and you don't remember how?" I scrunched my eyes and peered at her. "A bruise that size had to hurt...how could you *not* remember?"

"I bruise easily, and Mom says I'm spastic." She crossed her thin arms over her chest in a protective way. "I'm always falling and walking into things." A sound escaped from her mouth that would almost pass for a laugh, but she covered it with a fake cough while shrugging those thin shoulders again and jerking her skirt down over both knees to primly tuck the hem in tight.

"You sure are thin." My words gushed out before I could stop them. "Thinner than most models walking the catwalk...hey, you ever think about being a model?"

"Yeah, right." Her laugh sounded more genuine this time.

I nodded. "Seriously, you could wear anything with your thin body–actually, and I don't want you to take this the wrong way, you're a little *too* thin."

Elle jerked a finger to her lips. *"Shhh! Do NOT let Mom hear you say that!"*

Chapter 4

School Sucks

I suppose one could say I'm educationally challenged because most of my classes suck. If it wasn't for English Lit, my entire eighth grade would bottom out in the sewer. Truth is, even English Lit sucks, but it's my only class with Bryant Baker—not that he even knows I'm alive most of the time.

Bryant Baker is all things I am not–gorgeous hair, tremendous eyes, and super athletic. The only negative thing I could say about him is that he goes steady with Lexi Lanthrope, whose parents are Dr. Lanthrope and Dr. Lanthrope. Wonder if they call each other that at home? I can just see it now, 'Good morning, Dr. Lanthrope, how did you sleep? Fine, thank you, Dr. Lanthrope, and you'? Anyway, Bryant Baker is the only reason I can halfway stomach English Lit, even if he does have bad taste in girlfriends.

"Hey, watch where you're going, dummy!"

Speak of the Devil...I looked up in time to crash into, none other than, Lexi Lanthrope! "Err, sorry."

"Don't give me a description of your pitiful life." Lexi dusted off her shoulder where I bumped into her—as if I had lice. "Just get out of my way."

"Err, sorry," I repeated and side-stepped, giving her and her royal court the space they think they deserve.

Lexi Lanthrope is the most popular girl in school; captain of the cheer team and she and Bryant Baker have been going steady since sixth grade. Two years in a row, they got voted most popular *and* best-looking, (pardon me while I gag), and this year, she's determined to win Homecoming Queen. From the looks of things, her court is already in place if you count the two girls following her every step. I sneaked a look at them out of the corner of my eye as they giggled and whispered their way down the hall.

"Why do you let them treat you like that?"

I whirled to the sound of that voice. *It can't be!* "Elle? What are you doing here?"

An enhanced version of the skinny girl from dinner stood right in front of me with her once-lifeless hair now boasting a glossy shine ending in long curls (actually 'long bends') hanging down either side of a well made-up face softened with foundation and blush. Her dark eyes were framed by long black mascara lashes and pale pink lip gloss shimmered on her mouth. She still needed work to be called beautiful, but her appearance had improved a thousand percent from last night.

"What are you doing here?" I looked around to make sure I hadn't slipped into a parallel Universe.

Elle fluffed her bangs. "Mom just registered me here, and I'm now officially a student of dear old Mill Oak Junior High." She shook pretend pom-poms and executed a perfect high-kick. "*Go Trojans!*"

I grabbed her arm and yanked her toward the wall. "Elle, stop! You're embarrassing me! Are you crazy or something–everybody is looking at you."

"So, what if they are…aren't you allowed to show school spirit here?" She looked around at the other students already rushing to their next class, even making eye contact with a few of them.

Where's a hole in the floor when you need one? "What is going on inside your brain and why are you so overjoyed about transferring to school here? Aren't you the least bit upset about leaving your old school in New York?"

She shook her head. "No way. I'm just sorry we didn't move sooner, which by the way is official, or so Mom said last night–I don't ever have to go back to that place, not even to pack."

"Whoa, dude, what about all your stuff in New York?" I shifted my backpack from my left arm to my right.

"Dad will arrange for it to be packed up and shipped here—probably sometime today, or definitely as soon as we find a place to live."

We walked down the hall toward my next class. "So, your dad really will work with my dad, then?"

"Guess so." She checked the paper in her hand. "Say, where's Accounting II?"

I pointed toward a short hall. "Go down that way, turn left, and it's the first room on the left."

"Got it. See you at lunch." She almost skipped down the hall toward her first class as a Trojan.

I whooshed out a deep breath as I stared after this alien from last night, trying to wrap my head around what just happened before I remembered she doesn't have a clue where the Cafeteria is located. "Wait! I eat at 11:00—when do you go?"

Elle stopped and turned back toward me. "Same time. Mom made sure I got the same lunchtime as you…wish me luck."

"Good luck," I pointed over my shoulder, "and Cafeteria's back the other way, at the end of that long hall."

"No problem. I'll ask someone, and Amanda Jo, I'm so happy to be here!" Elle pumped her palms toward the ceiling and practically squealed the last word.

I shook my head and headed toward Math class, but two classes later, I went in search of Elle in the cafeteria. Might as well get the 'who's the new kid' question out of the way, but the one question that wouldn't get out of my way was who moves from New York to Iowa and is happy about it? I found the subject of my questions sitting alone at the first table.

"Amanda Jo. Over here."

Every eye in that room burned holes through me as I made my way over to where Elle sat. "Did you have to alert the Calvary? Everyone in here heard you."

"So? Why do I care?" Elle brushed her hair back from her face. "I was afraid you didn't see me."

"Oh, I saw you alright, everyone saw you." I made a big production of arranging the food on my tray. "So, where's your lunch?"

"I'm not hungry, so I dumped it in the trash, but I'll grab something later." She flicked a crumb from the table and her eyes followed its descent to the floor.

"Like dude, you don't eat anything. You're what…a size two?"

"Zero."

I almost choked on my Jell-O. "A zero? Who wears a size zero? Do they even make that size?" At size eleven, I was a gorilla compared to her.

"It's not a big deal, besides Mom makes me eat a huge dinner every night and if I'm not hungry, I have to sit at the table, like, forever."

Her mom must be Godzilla and Attila The Hun all rolled into one, and no way would I put up with that. "Mom made me sit at the table when I was, like, four…you want to come over after school?"

"Sure, but I'll have to check."

I wrinkled my nose. "Wait, you need to ask permission from your mom to just come over after school? You can't just text her, tell her you're going to my house, and that you'll let her know when you'll be home?"

Elle laughed. "Yeah, like you do that, and besides Mom might have plans for me to go house hunting after school, but this place is not bad for a lunchroom." She turned to look around the room. "Which ones are your friends?"

I did the only thing I could think of, I lied. "Most of my friends eat second lunch." Truth is my friends number on a scale of one to ten, a big whopping zero–same size as Elle's designer clothes.

"Well, it's a good thing I eat first lunch, then." Elle's eyes sparkled like two big stars in a black sky. She turned back around to look at the commotion going on at a nearby table and her elbow connected with her backpack, sending it flying to the floor. She jumped to pick it up, giving me my first good look at her matchy-matchy clothes.

Her jeans were stone-washed with pink flowers stitched along one seam from knee to hem. Her belt coordinated with her top, which was the same shade of pink as her hoodie. Her converses were neon green with pink laces, and the scarf around her neck had every color mentioned above.

That's an outfit I'd dress models in for a photo shoot if I had photo shoots or models. "I guess you didn't leave ALL your clothes behind since that outfit looks more New York than Midwest."

She propped her backpack against her leg. "Yeah well, I hate my clothes, because Mom picks out what she wants me to wear, not what I want to wear...even though she knows I prefer to, you know, fit in. Instead, I look like Mom's version of the well-dressed teen or something.

That's why I give them away...here, you want the scarf?"
She unwound the scarf from her neck and tossed it to me.
"Take it."

That's when I saw the second bruise.

Chapter 5

Houston...We Have A Problem

By Friday morning, even English Lit class couldn't pry my mind away from stressing about Elle. It was as if she had two personalities–the quiet little mouse at dinner that first night, and the hip, 'I don't give a flip', girl on the first day of school. One thing was for sure, though, both of them were hiding something.

What English Lit couldn't do, Bryant Baker could. Bryant sits in front of me in class and sometimes I stare at the little wisps of hair that curl up at the back of his neck and wonder what it would feel like to touch them. On a scale of one to ten, that would be a bazillion, three hundred million gazillion, five hundred and two trillion...

Somehow, I lived through my classes and headed to my locker where I emptied its entire contents into my backpack before trudging toward the front door and freedom. Just steps away from the big escape, I felt someone breathing down my neck.

Lexi Lanthrope eased up behind me and tugged my ponytail hard. "So, who's your weird little friend in the lunchroom yesterday—she must be new here; otherwise, she wouldn't share a table with you." She wrinkled her nose. "Won't be for long. Soon as she gets downwind, she'll find herself another table."

I attempted to walk away, but Lexi jostled around me to poke her face into mine. "All nerds smell alike." She fanned her nose. "Eau de puke."

"Hey, Amanda Jo." Bryant Baker called from his locker near the front door. "Lexi, Jennifer…you all need to cool it. You're not funny, you know." He shoved books into his locker. "See you after practice, girlfriend." He gave Lexi a playful punch on the cheek, but the colossal news is he *winked* at *me*. "Bye, Amanda Jo."

I died right there, and if nothing else good ever happens to me my entire life, it's okay. I tossed my ponytail, smiled at the two Lexi wannabees, and sashayed toward the front door, practically gliding without ever once touching the floor.

Lexi's voice screeched after me like grinding glass. "Did you see that? Bryant winked at Miss Butt-Ugly—what was he thinking? Like, you wait 'til I see him after practice."

Jennifer's voice drifted through the open door. "Ignore him. He was probably making fun of her…she is to be pitied, you know."

Butt-ugly? That's not the message I received. My grin grew ear-to-ear as I kept on trucking it outside through the front door into a glorious sunshiny world where the birds sang, the breeze beckoned, and the trees whispered my name. On a scale of one to ten, well, that wink was off the charts.

I sailed through the rest of the afternoon and night by reliving those twenty seconds at Bryant's locker. Nothing Earth-shattering as a wink had ever happened before, but he had once looked in my direction and smiled. Now, my entire being, my reason to live, centered around that one wink, and I was still sparkling inside—bright as a neon sign flashing SALE!—when Mom dropped Elle and me off at the mall the next morning.

As soon as we waved goodbye to Mom, Elle turned to me and demanded, "You look like you're going to bust a gut. Come on girlfriend, *SPILL!*"

"It's nothing...just the coolest boy in school winked at me yesterday, and right in front of his girlfriend, to boot."

Elle wore dark blue skinny jeans and a Bohemian top that I'd not seen before, and she almost looked normal—even her Converses were 'everybody's got a pair' black. "So that made you spaz out?"

"Yesterday it was huge, but then I realized it doesn't mean a thing because today, he's still got a girlfriend. On top of that, he's popular and popular guys don't go out with nobodies–they go out with doctor's kids."

"Who says you're a nobody?" Elle demanded.

"Everyone. Look, forget Bryant Baker. Let's check out the arcade."

Elle stopped, crammed her fists into her side, and screeched, "Bryant Baker? *OhMyGosh!* Like, he's the big basketball star—no wonder you're grinning like you discovered America, but doesn't he go with that witch Lexi 'Lollipop'. Wait! Isn't Lexi your archenemy—Like. Batman. And. The. Penguin?"

"She better not hear you call her that; besides like he'd ever give me the time of day, anyway."

"He would so *too* give you the time of day." Elle linked her arm through mine and tugged me down the mall. "Look at you—you've got a great figure, not skin and bones like me, and your hair doesn't just hang there like a string–plus, you're funny and you look like everybody else and fit in."

I rolled my eyes. "Yeah right, exactly all the things a big basketball star wants in a girlfriend...*NOT!* Dude seriously, drop it, and let's go score some fries and a coke, and then we need to hook you up with some nude lip gloss."

Elle stopped short. "*O.M.G!* Did you see that?" Her voice squeaked like a trapped mouse.

"What, where, who?" We'd just passed the arcade where a gang of boys huddled around the foosball table, and I figured whatever Elle saw must involve them, so I stopped and stared.

Elle pivoted me around like a Popsicle on a stick. "Not that way—look over there, the TEEN SCENE shop." She tilted her neck toward the block of shops where all my classmates hung out. She whispered, "None other than Lexi 'Lollipop' and her gang of girl goof-offs." Her head pointed straight ahead, but her eyes struck right angles so no one would know where she was looking.

I strained to see what had caught her attention, but she yanked me forward by my shirttail causing me to miss my step and stumble to the ground. The material of my favorite shirt ripped like opening a zipper from the bottom to about halfway up the side seam and now hung at odd angles. "What is up with you? You can't just act like a goon over somebody being at the same mall as you—it's a free country, right? Even Lexi and her clowns can shop at the mall, *right?*"

This strange person who stood beside me kept staring across the mall. Was she hallucinating or maybe hunger deprived her of brain cells.

"Look, let's go eat." I attempted to walk off, but Elle's fingers dug into my right arm, causing me to wince in pain. I swung around, and with a serious jerk of my arm, broke her death-grip. "You do that again and I'm out of here like slime on a dime."

Elle's eyes bore into mine and her death grip found its way back to my arm stronger than ever. "No! I just saw Lexi cram something into her purse, like, a sweater or something." Her voice cackled halfway between a creak and a croak—almost as if she had a piece of candy stuck in her windpipe. *"She just shop-lifted something!"*

The hair on my arms stood up and paid attention, causing a shiver to scuttle down my spine. "No way, you're kidding, right?" Then totally unmindful of her hand still anchored to my arm, I swiveled my head in the direction of the store but saw nothing. "You're sure it was Lexi?" I squinted my eyes to scan deeper inside, but still saw nothing to incriminate the drama queen of all queens, so I peered back at Elle in time to see her head bob up and down.

Elle's eyes were the size of potato chips. "Sure as I'm standing here. Let's go check it out." She pulled me along with her.

I did another rotating one-eighty with my arm to break Elle's grip. "Go inside there? No way, Jose." Now, it was *me* trying to get *her* not to look toward the store. "Stop looking at them, don't even think about going into that store because I'm definitely not, and neither should you."

She grabbed my arm again and even though I dug my heels in, she bump-bumped me along a step or two.

"Elle, I told you I'm not going anywhere near them—I don't even like them, so what do I care if they get in trouble?" Suddenly, my stomach somersaulted, and my mouth soured with bile—Lexi Lanthrope has that effect on me. "Let's go get a Coke or something. My treat."

Elle plastered her gaze back on me, her eyes twinkling like Christmas lights on steroids. "They don't have to see us—we just go make sure it was Lexi who did the shop-lifting and then we'll walk away. No harm, no foul."

I darted a look toward the store, which I'm sure was a sign of weakness. "Let's say I believe you, let's say it was

Lexi, and let's say she did just what you said she did...why should *we* be the ones to confront her when we see her ugly face five days a week? *I* sure don't need to spend Saturday morning looking at it, too, but if you are so inclined, be my guest."

"Come on, Amanda Jo...we go in, we tell her we know what's in her bag, and then we leave, so the next time she smart-mouths you, you remind her about the sweater and threaten to spill the beans. It's called leverage."

One eyebrow skated up, and without a word, I turned on my heel and followed Elle across the mall to the shop–biggest mistake of my life.

Chapter 6

Pictures, Glasses, Me, and Other Things That Get Framed

Elle steered me through the entrance of a shop overflowing with tees in all shapes and patterns from Tie-dyed, sling-back, off-the-shoulder, screen-printed, neon, and plain. I couldn't help but check out a few as we walked by, but Elle soon yanked me along like we were on some sort of a mission. I guess we were.

"Dude!" I said with more force than intended, "stop pulling me."

Elle's lips emitted a shushing sound as she pointed to the back of the store where a mix of giggles and whispers saturated the air. A white-blond head popped into view and Elle pulled me down behind a rack of jeans.

"It *is* Lexi," she whispered. "Don't let her see you."

Panic hurled my heart into a gallop. *"Now can we go?"*

Elle jumped to her feet and pulled me up beside her. "On second thought, let's stroll by and let her know we're onto her." She yanked me forward.

I sideswiped a pocketbook tree that launched its contents all over the hardwood floor, totally blowing my attempt at stealth-mode, and garnering me dirty looks from a sales clerk. I bit my lip, slumped my shoulders, and tailed Elle toward the trio.

"Who said dorks could shop here?" Lexi's greeting made my skin crawl. She's even nasty in public.

Unlike me, Elle straightened her shoulders. "Oh, it's okay for you to be here–I checked the rules."

A choking breath caught hard in my chest. Coughing and sputtering, I spat out, "Come on, Elle, let's get out of here before they get us in trouble." This time, I tugged on *her* shirt.

Elle shook me off like last week's news. "Hang on a sec...we've got as much right to be here as them, and besides I'd like to see what all Lexi Lollipop just crammed into her bag– which I'm sure she fully intends to pay for." Her eyes gripped Lexi's in a death stare.

My mouth bottomed out like a runaway elevator, black spots shaded my vision, and my stomach threatened to toss its cookies.

"Get lost, creep." Lexi shouldered herself between Elle and me.

Elle shoved back. "You get lost, freak."

I stared dumbfounded, as if aliens processed my body, while the two of them pushed and shoved, slapped, and clawed behind the rack of jeans.

The next scene was right out of a horror movie as Lexi grabbed Elle by her hair and spun her around while, in return, Elle elbowed Lexi in the stomach. Both of them fell backward through the jeans rack.

Finally, snapping out of my stupor, I jumped to Elle's rescue and the next thing I knew, Lexi snaked out a hand, grabbed me by my backpack, and yanked me behind the same rack of jeans.

Clawing, scratching hands pinned me down, and even though I gave it my all to break free, I might as well have been in a straight-jacket. After that, everything became a blur until someone or something tugged hard on my backpack.

"Hey, let go!" I jerked my bag, but not before Lexi crammed something inside. Twisting and turning, kicking and scratching, the embattled scene quickly turned into a war zone with Lexi and her goons having the upper hand, leaving me no option short of a super-hero to get out of there alive.

Finally, Lexi pulled me to my feet only to shove me backward, again. Her voice rose to a level that could be heard in the next county. "Do you intend to pay for that or did you just shop-lift that yellow sweater?"

My right ankle rolled, and with nothing but air to grab onto, I fell for what seemed like two minutes and would have smacked the floor had that same clerk from the pocketbook fiasco not rushed toward us, eyes glaring and, I could have sworn, steam whistling from her ears.

The lady grabbed my arm. "All right, missy…what's going on here?"

Not yet sure of my footing, I careened to the floor, pitching headfirst, while the clerk rendered another futile attempt to catch me, but snagged my backpack instead, jerking it from my shoulder.

The contents tumbled out onto the clerk's shiny black pumps, including a new item—the ugliest yellow sweater I'd ever seen, still attached to the price tag.

"Oh, my." The clerk's voice mimicked a foghorn.

I blinked several times to clear my vision, only to zone in on her face, a face boasting the deepest frown I'd ever seen.

Her eyes, two beady black buttons on either side of her nose, glared down at me. "I *know* what's going on."

My mouth worked, but nothing came out as my voice failed me and cobwebs filled me—filled my head at least, and on top of that, my eyes kept drifting south as if it were time for my afternoon siesta. More than likely, my condition bordered on convulsion, no, a connection, or a concussion—one of those words that begin with a 'C'.

"Come with me, young lady." The clerk firmly grasped my arm, weaving me in and out of clothes racks to propel me toward an open doorway at the back of the shop. She clutched my backpack in her free hand, with the yucky yellow sweater, compliments of Lexi Lanthrope, hanging half-in, half-out.

My eyes darted to the clerk's face, which looked darker than dirt. "I want to go home, please let me go home…are you calling the police? Wait, I can't go to jail—

don't take me to jail, because I'm too young to go to jail, and besides, Mom will be mad if I go to jail!"

Lexi dogged our footsteps. "I saw her do it, ma'am, and it's just not right, you know—not when the rest of us have to save our allowance and babysitting money just to buy nice things. She should have to wait until she can afford it, like the rest of us."

I stared into Lexi's lying eyes only to see a satisfied smirk plastered there and my mouth fell open at how calmly she had accused me of stealing—when she was the actual culprit! I darted another glance back to the clerk. "Can't you see she's lying?" Hot anger hit my body like a bulldozer, but water might as well have coursed through my veins, for all the good it did me, because the clerk paid no attention to my words, nor did she relax her hold on my arm.

Lexi waved a putrid goodbye, whirled on the heel of one expensive leather boot, and strutted her merry band of thieves safely out of the store. On a scale of one to ten, my luck clouted zero.

The clerk dragged me into a tiny office that belonged to 'R. Davis, Manager', pushed me into a seat and pointed a finger in my face. "Stay put." She slammed the door behind her and the click-click-click of her heels carried her away.

I knew I was in a heap of trouble now, and Mom would probably ground me for life, kill me dead, take away my phone, Internet, and movies—in other words, life, as I knew it, was over. I could forget moving to New York and becoming a fashion designer. Heck, I could forget finishing high school since I'd probably spend every waking hour in my dumb room over that dumb funeral home for the rest of my dumb days.

"Amanda Jo!"

I jerked around to see Elle's face in the cracked doorway. "Elle!" I pole-vaulted the desk, flung myself on her thin body, and would have bawled right then and there if she hadn't clamped her hand over my mouth.

"Shhhh! Come on."

I didn't wait for an explanation. I jogged after Elle down a back hallway, through an emergency exit, and out into bright sunshine where we pounded the pavement as we tore around the building, across the parking lot, and across the freeway. We didn't stop until we reached the park on the other side of the street.

I butted up to a tree and bent over double with a stitch in my side the size of Mount Rushmore, and even though I gasped for air through my wide-open mouth, freedom had never felt so good. It took several seconds before I could speak, but when I could, I thanked Elle over and over. "Thank you, thank you, thank you! You totally saved my life! I would be sleeping in a jail cell tonight if you hadn't rescued me, but where did you go? Last I saw, you disappeared through a rack of jeans."

Elle's skinny body sprawled onto the hard ground, her chest double-timing as fast as mine. "Lexi's goons held me down on the floor, then one of them sat on me, and the other one went to work on you. You wait until I get my hands on them—I'll strangle them, then go home and eat ice cream…no banana pudding, and maybe ice cream, too."

I laughed despite my aching chest. "And I'll help you eat ice cream and banana pudding, speaking of which, I never did get that coke." I slid down the tree trunk and landed with a plop on the ground and wiped the sweat from my eyes. "But can you believe Lexi? She's *so* not a nice person, and if it's the last thing I do, I'll get her for what she did—I get traipsed to the manager's office while she dances out of the store with who knows what in her greedy little hands…talk about unfair." I turned my head so Elle couldn't see the tears that, all of a sudden, stung my eyes.

Why Lexi? She had everything in the world anyone could ever want, and now steals what she doesn't have? On a scale of one to ten, that sucked air off the charts, even though I *had* managed to escape, thanks to Elle, and that counts for something.

"Amanda Jo!" Elle jerked into a sitting position. *"Where's your backpack?"*

Chapter 7

Heat Wave

I managed to squeak through the remainder of the weekend by pretending to be sick–which was not a big stretch at all, since I could have easily thrown up every time I remembered how close I came to going to jail. If the store contacts Mom about the lost backpack, I may still wind up in an orange jumpsuit with an industrial-sized ankle bracelet as my only accessory.

Mentally, I examined the contents of my backpack and ticked off the list on my fingers to include lotus blossom lip gloss, twelve dollars and change, a door key on a purple-braided key chain, a purple gel pen, and a new journal. Luckily, I hadn't written in it, yet, but for the life of me, I couldn't remember if I had inked in any personal contact info or not.

The rest of the inventory included two purple scrunchies and a half-eaten candy bar because you never know when you might need chocolate, but the one thing I beat myself up over was last week's newspaper article showing Bryant Baker's winning two points in the game against State. *All the better to determine your school, my dear.*

"Hey, A.J." Elle's voice broke my concentration, so I slammed my locker door and turned to see her weaving through the crowd.

I tossed a quick glance around to see if you-know-who was within earshot. "My name's not A.J."

"Is to me." She hooked a finger in one of my belt loops, pulled me to the wall, and leaned close, her brows almost touching in the middle. "So, any calls about your backpack?"

"Not yet." I looked nervously, once again, up and down the hall. "Maybe it'll all fizzle out and go away. Like maybe someone found it and tossed it in the garbage by now." I hoped, anyway.

"Yeah, like that's going to happen when it's a link to a shop-lifting gang." Elle's outfit choice of the day consisted of khakis and sweatshirt with a button-up underneath; polished, cute, and glam–all synced into one, but the temperature bordered on 75 degrees outside, a late fall heatwave.

"I'm not a shop-lifting gang–neither are you, but as far as that clerk is concerned, neither is Lexi. Aren't you burning up in that outfit?" I glanced around at the herd traveling the hallway, some pushing and rushing, others strolling as if they had nowhere to go, but most sporting short sleeves.

"Mom says I'm cold-natured." She shook her hair out of her eyes. "You done?"

I faced my locker but sidewaysed a look at Elle, who didn't look cold-natured to me. She looked hot, if anything. "Got to grab another book or two." I scanned the locker's contents before deciding I had what I needed before asking, "Want to go get something to eat at Charley's?"

Elle shifted from one foot to the other. "Can't because we're moving today, and I thought maybe you'd come help me fix up my new room."

I jerked around. "For real?"

"For real." Her smile said it all.

"Sweet. What time?"

"Mom says they'll have the last load there by the time I get out of school, so now, I guess."

"How's about I meet you there in an hour, then?" I high-fived her on my way out the door.

Mom agreed to drop me off, and I stared out the window as we breezed down the highway toward Elle's new home. My thoughts, as always, drifted to THE PLAN, a plan I perfected in my mind on a daily basis. I would get my permit in two years and my full-fledged license a year after that, and then I was well on my way to blowing this Popsicle stand. Each birthday promised big changes to my life. I'd been promised a car when I turned sixteen, but you never knew how many ways Mom might find to renege on her word; and besides, I'm not a perfect child, you know–I do mess up from time to time.

We cruised down the by-pass toward Elle's house, and I flashed a look at Mom. "Like, you know what kind of car I want for my birthday in three years, right?"

"A Mustang." She gripped the steering wheel with one hand and dug around on the inside of her purse with the other one.

"What color?"

"Blue."

"Just making sure you haven't forgotten." I smiled.

Mom pulled out her lipstick. "Not forgotten, but not planning on it, either." She smeared a line across her bottom lip and smacked them to even the color.

"Mom! Everyone gets a car when they get their driver's license."

"You're not everyone."

"Tell me about it." I clenched my teeth. "Let me clarify, EVERYONE ELSE gets a car when they turn sixteen, everyone except me."

"Well, then everyone else should be happy, and besides, it's not my responsibility to make sure you're happy all the time, just well-fed and loved." Mom smiled that sickly-sweet smile of hers and tossed the lipstick back in her purse. "Is this our turn?"

Game, point, match.

I gawked at the three-story mansions on either side of the street, each one boasting a nice long circular driveway. "Wow, they bought a house here? They must have tons of money, and I bet Elle gets a *new* car when she turns sixteen."

"Stop obsessing about other people and concentrate on yourself and your family. We don't base our lives on what other people have or have not. Let's see…it's the fourth house past the Masons." She clicked off the houses. "One, two, three, four... there, it must be that driveway with the fountain."

"Holy crap!"

Mom's eyes threw daggers at me. "Watch it, pottymouth, we do not use that word ever, or I'll be scrubbing your mouth out with soap when you get home."

"I'm sorry, it just slipped out, and you know I don't use that word ever, but I certainly wouldn't use it if I get a car when I turn sixteen."

Mom threw me a look and flipped on the blinker. She nosed the car into the large driveway, up to a three-car garage with open doors stuffed full of boxes that were overflowing inside and spilling to the outside.

I lowered my window. "Hey, Elle!"

"A.J.!" Elle dropped the box she held and waved.

Mom opened her door and poked her head out. "Hello, Elle—love your new house." She turned to me. "And who's A.J.?"

"That'd be me, I guess." I swung out of the car.

"You need to tell her your name is Amanda Jo." Mom's frowny-face was firmly in place. "You know I don't tolerate nicknames."

"I didn't care for it either, at first; but after a while, it tends to grow on you."

Mom's frown turned sour as she slammed the car door. "So does bacteria if you stop bathing, and just because someone else does it, doesn't mean you allow it."

Her frown turned into a smile when she caught sight of Mrs. Chambers. "Oh hi, Amy. Pretty day for moving."

So, it was okay for Mrs. Chambers to use a nickname, but apparently, there was a different set of rules for me.

Mrs. Chambers, decked out in a yellow tank top and matching jeans, waved from the front porch. Her hair, sleeked back in a ponytail, portrayed her to be closer to my age than Mom's. On a scale of one to ten, Mom was a low two, while Mrs. Chambers was a ten, even on moving day.

"Want to come in?" Mrs. Chambers asked.

Mom held her position by the car. "Not this time. I'm only dropping off reinforcements, but I'll be back to pick her up before supper–say around six?"

"Oh, let her stay." Mrs. Chambers smiled. "We'll probably order pizza, and I'll run her home around eight–okay?"

Mom turned to me. "What about homework?"

"Don't got none."

"'Don't got none'." Mom shook her head. "Keep that up, missy, and you'll have English homework EVERY night–I'll see to it."

"I meant to say I don't have any homework that needs to be finished tonight." I rolled my eyes at Elle and wondered how in the world she could stand to wear that heavy sweatshirt–especially unpacking boxes.

Mom waved again at Mrs. Chambers. "Okay, if you're sure…"

"We'll be fine." Mrs. Chambers nodded.

I waved at Mom as she backed out of the driveway and felt my stomach growl, and even though I'd eaten all my lunch at school, I knew I'd sure be able to put away my share of that pizza.

"What kind of pizza do you want, girls?" Mrs. Chambers linked an arm through mine as we walked back to where Elle stood nudging a half-empty box with her toe.

"Don't care." Elle's thin shoulders attempted to shrug, but with the heavy shirt, the movement was barely visible.

"Amanda Jo?" Mrs. Chambers fixed her eyes on me.

"We usually order from Hal's Pizza on Thomas. I've got the number programmed into my cell and can order for you if you want."

"That would be great." Mrs. Chambers headed upstairs and into what seemed to be a kitchen. "Tell them the address is 242 Michael's Boulevard, and I'll be right back with the money—what, twenty-five bucks, pizza, and tip?"

I tallied numbers in my head. "Probably, but I'll let you know." My eyes swooped down on a box containing a dozen or so pairs of shoes. "Whoa! These are to-die-for— has New York City called asking for their missing box of shoes for Fashion Week, yet?" I grabbed the navy and tan wedges.

Elle's eyes never found mine. "Keep them and there's a matching belt around here somewhere." Her hair, also pulled back in a ponytail, sprung wispy curls that decorated her face—a face drenched with sweat.

"You're sweating like a majorette in a Fourth of July parade—why don't you shed that heavy shirt. It has to be 100 degrees in here."

"Get off my back about the freakin' shirt, will you?" Elle burst into tears and tore out of the garage.

Chapter 8

Queen of Denial

By the time the pizza arrived, I had piled all the shoes back into the box and carried it, and two more boxes marked 'Elle', to the kitchen door. I figured it would be best to go through them in her room. That way, she could keep what she wanted and leave the rest in the box for throwing away, yard sale, or donation. I watch TV–I know how you're supposed to clean out closets: one pile for keeping, one pile for donating, one pile for dumping.

Mrs. Chambers lugged a card table into the garage, and I set it up while she returned to the kitchen to grab three soft drinks. When she returned, she looked around. "Where's Elle?"

"Uh, she, uh, hauled something to her room." I lied, even though I knew better–but Elle didn't appear to like her mom very much, so why should I?

Mrs. Chambers laughed. "I'll call her cell. Whatever did we do before cell phones?" Her blue eyes sparkled, sending a shiver skipping down my spine. That must be what Mom means by a 'cold chill'. My mind kept jumping back to Elle. I couldn't help but wonder if now was a good time for me to go home, or should I go check on my new friend.

"Elle honey, pizza's here. You need to come down and keep your little friend company, honey."

If she says 'honey' once more, I'm going to puke.

"No, your dad will be home later. We'll get the mess cleaned up long before he gets home. Hurry up, let's eat." She opened the box and reached it out to me. "You first. Elle's coming down."

I did go first, only because I was hungry, and only because this was my favorite pizza, and only because I trusted the people who cooked it. The jury was still out on Mrs. Chambers.

Elle finally joined us and took the smallest piece of pizza in the box. She gulped her soft drink and crammed the pizza in her mouth without making eye contact with me as if she had only so much time to choke the pizza down. No matter how hard I tried, I couldn't figure her out.

After two pieces of pizza (me, definitely not the other two), Elle and I decided we'd tote the shoebox up to her room—a room I'd yet to see. "So, can you lift your side?"

"Probably." Elle's eyes never once met mine.

For some unknown reason, she decided we'd go around and through the front door, by-passing her mom in the kitchen. We dragged the box up the two steps to the front porch. Once inside, we scooted the box on the plush pale pink carpet—who installs pale pink carpet? Rich people who can afford to have it cleaned every month, I guess; and those with very little design taste.

Elle's room was at the back of the house on the second floor. We pulled and pushed the box up the hardwood steps, down the hardwood floor, and into the room at the back of the hall–a room with the same pink carpet as downstairs. At least the walls were white.

"Nice room." I looked around at the A-framed ceiling, which reminded me of last summer's vacation cabin in Maine–only this room was completely void of wood paneling.

"It's okay."

"Look, you want me to call Mom to come get me?" I felt as if I was in the way or something.

"No." Elle's face looked as bewildered as I felt. "Why do you want to leave?"

I raked the hair out of my eyes. "I don't know what's going on with you, today." I shifted from one foot to the other. "You wanted me to come and now you don't seem happy I'm here–heck, you don't even seem happy *you're* here; and you're the one that wanted to move to 'Boring Town', Iowa, in the first place. You change your mind? Cause I totally understand if you have, I don't want to live here either, remember?"

"No, I'm glad we moved here." She delivered her signature move: shoulders shrugging for all get out. "I just want my room fixed up."

"What's not fixed up about this place?" My eyes joined hers in a wrestling match.

"Well, not fixed up exactly. Like, everything put in its place, you know?" She gestured to the boxes on the floor.

I rose to my feet. "If you'll get off your can and help me, we'll get it done."

She cut me off. "Never mind. Let's just shove that whole box into the closet for now, out of sight, and then we can hang up those clothes." She gestured toward the bed.

I looked at my new friend. Where's the happy girl from school?

After several pilgrimages from bed to the closet, I realized I was working alone. "Elle?" I stepped backward and craned my neck around the wall to look into the adjoining bathroom, the 'ensuite', I think they call it.

The door, cracked slightly, afforded me a clear sightline to Elle bent over the commode. Her fingers disappeared deep down her throat. What in the world was she doing? I watched for several seconds and then stared in amazement as Elle vomited her entire slice of pizza, and then some. I read about that. Binge and purge. Only Elle never binged.

I lofted the hangers toward the closet, uncaring if they landed on the floor, and tried to erase the scene from my mind, but I couldn't.

Elle strolled out of the bathroom, wiping her mouth with her sleeve as if nothing had happened.

I rushed to the closet to rescue the clothes I'd tossed on the floor. "What now?" My heart pounded. My head tried to absorb what I'd just seen: my only friend in the whole world was anorexic; of that, I was positive. Binge and Purge...is that Elle's way of dealing with her family? Was she really upset about moving or was she jealous of her mother?

"Guess we could make my bed." Elle opened another box to pull out pink and green sheets, curtains, and pillows.

"At least, your stuff matches the carpet." My smile was genuine despite the tension in the room.

"It just came today. Mom ordered it to match. I could care less."

I dug deep in the box to lift out the gingham bed skirt in pink, green, and white with long lacy ruffles. "Lucky." I ran a hand over the colorful material. The closest I'd come to having something that matched was if both pillowcases were the same color.

"No. Guilty conscious."

Now, I considered throwing up. Part of me didn't want to know what Elle meant by that statement; but deep-down, another part did. The bruises–does Elle's mother beat her, then buy stuff to make up for it? Is that what Elle meant by a guilty conscience? And, like, what business is it of mine, anyway?

I snagged a deep breath. "Look, if you want to talk about it, I'll listen and won't make jokes." Heck, I really wanted to run and not learn any dirty little secrets about the Chambers family; but Elle was my friend, my only friend.

"Nothing to tell." Her eyes never looked up while she pulled at a thread in her jeans. "It's just life."

"Doesn't have to be." I tossed the bed skirt aside and dug deeper into the box, mindlessly pulling out pillows in every shape and size. "You think your mom went a little overboard?"

"She tends to do that." She shrugged those thin shoulders again. "Why do you think I have clothes coming out of my ying-yang?" She plopped down on the unmade bed, shoes and all, sending the brightly colored sheets cascading to the floor. "Like that makes everything even."

I flung the pillow back into the box and rushed to the bed, stomach-churning for sure now, but I pushed on. "Elle, what *is* wrong. You can tell me. I'm on your side."

For a brief moment, a look flickered across her face. A look I didn't recognize. *Is she going to cry?*

Suddenly she jumped up, crossed her arms over her chest, and plastered her goofy grin back in place. Then grabbing the sheets, she tossed a corner to me. "Hey, you dork, nothing's wrong, except we haven't made this bed. If we don't get it done, I'll have to sleep on the floor tonight. Grab that end and go around."

Numbly, I followed her instructions. Whatever was wrong, it must be something she was scared to talk about. Even to me.

As Elle tucked the sheet over her side of the mattress, the heavy sweatshirt rose a few inches above her belt, exposing an ugly red whelp on her back.

"Dang, what happened to you?" Impulsively, I reached out a hand.

"Leave me alone! Don't touch me! Get out! I hate you!" She collapsed to the floor, sobbing, and retching loudly.

Mrs. Chambers burst into the room and fell across her broken daughter. Gathering Elle in her arms, she rocked and cooed, uttering sounds I'd never heard before.

Tears stung my eyes as I watched a woman I didn't know, cuddle and rock her daughter I couldn't understand.

I crept downstairs and called Mom.

Chapter 9

Metamorphosis

"So what happened to Amy bringing you home at eight?" Mom pulled out into traffic.

I stared out my window and grunted.

"Did something happen?"

"No. I just ate my pizza and was ready to come home. Besides, I remembered I do have homework, after all." The homework card usually always worked.

"Amanda Jo. How could you forget about homework? You need to march up to your room and get it finished before your bath. I don't like it when you throw our schedule off."

Elle missed several days at school. I wondered if she'd left town, contracted an infectious disease, or was just avoiding me. Not only didn't she answer my text messages, but she also refused to pick up my calls–who knew what was going on over at that house. Maybe Elle's mom freaked or something, or Elle doesn't like me anymore, or she possibly lost her cell phone, or even *maybe* I'd dreamed the entire Elle story–just another screwed-up possibility in my screwed-up life. If that last scenario was true, that dream, on a scale of one to ten, would be the same size as our national debt.

I even Googled 'bruises' once and learned Elle could have anything from a simple trauma to the body to leukemia! I sure hoped it wasn't leukemia, but Elle could be dying with cancer and didn't want anyone to know. Maybe her mom showers her with presents because she only has a short time to live. Maybe it's none of my business, and I need to back off.

I saw Mr. Chambers a few times but didn't ask any questions. Surely, he knew what was happening with his daughter in her own home, but if Elle *was* being abused, how could any dad let someone beat his daughter, even if it was his own wife doing the beating?

I just couldn't wrap my head around the abuse thing–especially since they had money. I mean, they looked good, they lived good, and they acted good. Both parents graduated college.

I read once about a poor uneducated family who never had enough food to eat. The dad was a drunk and beat his children. Nothing about that story fit Elle's family. It had to be cancer.

School still sucked, but without Elle to talk to, the days fell back into the same boring routine as before. Like the morning I walked into the bathroom at school and came face-to-face with the *chosen ones.*

"Get out, dork!" Lexi heaved a roll of toilet paper toward my face. I had the good sense to duck. The roll missed my face, bounced off the wall, and unfurled down the length of the room, trailing a long skinny white carpet across the floor. "Now look what you did!"

"Public bathroom." Whoa, I just stood up to the great Lexi Lanthrope. A tiny grin pulled at my mouth as I headed toward a stall, but one of her goons beat me to it and blocked my path. "Get out of my way." My voice sounded calm to my ears, but inside my chest, a mist morphed into a mighty storm, threatening to burst any moment.

"Get out of OUR bathroom." Goon Number 1 thrust her fists on her hips, ponytail swinging up and down, making her look like a Bobblehead.

"Yeah, dorkster, get out of OUR bathroom." Goon Number 2 joined in.

I almost turned on my heel and walked out, *almost*–but not this time. This time, a new energy emerged, and I stared the three girls down, mostly because I had no idea what else to do. Then I heard these words tumble out of my mouth: "I have as much right to be here as you." Almost instantaneously, my back stiffened and I tossed Lexi a look. "You don't own this bathroom–you can't shoplift something this big, now can you?" Heck yeah, that newfound defiance felt pretty darn good.

Lexi bolted over to shove her nose in my face. "What did you say, dork?" Her eyes scowled like burnt coals, red spots exploded on her cheeks, and scorching hot breath stung my eyes.

I should have been scared, but all I could think about was 'Bozo, the clown'. I snorted with laughter without really intending to, which only made the red spots expand. I cleared my throat and drew a deep breath. My back stiffened even more, and I towered to my full five feet, four inches. "I said you can't shoplift the bathroom like you did that sweater at the mall." Once my mouth opened, the words wouldn't stop. It was as if I had diarrhea of the mouth or a volcano had erupted inside me and the lava-words poured out. Something akin to joy leaped up inside me and tickled my nose before exploding into fluttering butterflies.

For once, Lexi and her goons were speechless.

By now, I couldn't shut up if I wanted to. I didn't. "I told them, you know." I crossed fingers on both hands behind my back, knowing I'd regret lying later. "They know your parents' names, where you live, and your phone numbers. Any day now, the police will hunt you down, might even come to school, and arrest all three of you. I *so* wouldn't want to be you right now." I snorted again before realizing here I am, outnumbered three to one, and my mouth cannot stop spewing words. Maybe I'm the Bozo.

Before Lexi could respond, the door opened, and we jerked apart. All of a sudden, I didn't need to 'go' after all; instead, I rushed out the door without looking back and didn't stop until I saw who stood in front of my locker.

"Hey A.J."

"Elle! Where have you been all week?"

"I had strep. Miss me?" The new Elle was back.

"I thought you were dead or maybe moved again."

"Why is your face so red?" She flicked a finger toward my cheek.

"Oh, nothing." I smacked her hand away. "Just Lexi and her goons in the bathroom just now."

Elle grabbed my arm. "Come on, let's go have a word with Miss Lexi Lollipop."

I dug my heels into the tiled floor. "Elle, don't! Let it go—it won't help. Besides, I told her."

"Told her what?"

"Told her I turned her in. To the mall police."

She loosened her grip on my arm, but she didn't relinquish it. "You didn't, did you? Oh, what does it matter anyway? People like her never get in trouble. Only people like me. And you. Aren't you tired of taking crap from people?" She exhaled, finally dropping her hand. "I know I am." She visibly wilted right before my eyes. "Forget it."

Goodbye, new Elle. I watched my friend skulk down the hall, knowing her situation was far worse than mine. I don't live with Lexi. I only have to avoid her during the day. Elle can't run away from her family, but I resolved to find a way to help her, even if it takes my last dying breath.

It almost did.

Chapter 10

Rebirth

Mill Oak Junior High's basketball team plays their arch-rival tonight. I normally don't attend games, but Elle pressured me, and I decided I'd sacrifice this one time. Watching Bryant Baker play basketball had nothing to do with my decision, I told myself. *Yeah, right!* I answered.

Mom pulled into the Chambers' driveway and Elle yanked open the door and lunged into the back seat before Mom completely stopped the car.

"Well, hello. You're ready to go, I guess." Mom looked at Elle in the rear-view.

I quickly forgot about the game when I zeroed in on the sick expression plastered across Elle's face. She was as white as Casper, the friendly ghost; but there was nothing friendly about her appearance. Terrified, maybe. She visibly shook. Her body coiled tighter than a flat Slinky. It was as if any minute she would spiral straight up, circle the moon, and crash-land in the neighbor's pool. Come to think of it, I'd seen that look on her face before.

Elle said nothing, her eyes locked on the front door of her house.

Simultaneously, my mouth watered, and my throat closed; choking and sputtering, I feared I'd barf, for sure, if anyone opened that front door. I darted a look at Mom. Surely, she's suspicious. Without saying a word, I pleaded with Elle: *Act normal.*

"I like your hair," I blurted.

Actually, Elle's hair looked really nice tonight. Hopefully, Mom would focus on that. On how nice Elle looked. Her hair was pulled back in a high ponytail, making her eyes pop more than usual.

Or was that fear?

"Thanks." Elle never met my stare. A thin line slashed across her face where her mouth normally hung, her eyes fastened on that front door.

Mom turned around. "Everything okay, dear?" I could see a wrinkle across her forehead. Not a good sign.

"Fine." Elle nodded. "Can we just go?" Panic tugged at her face and oozed from her frail frame.

My heart flip-flopped. We were in for it now. Mom would never mind her own business. She wouldn't budge until Elle spilled her guts, and I already knew what happened when that dam breaks. Elle could start shrieking any second.

"You're absolutely sure your parents are good with you going to the ballgame, right?" Mom continued to study Elle in the rear-view.

I darted another look to the front door, insides churning, praying: Please, please, please God. Don't let Elle's mom come out. "Mom, can we just go? We're late already, and I didn't spend all week deciding what to wear to be late for the game, you know? Besides, who wants to walk in late in front of the whole crowd?" I did my best to sound flip, like nothing was up, but the world could come crashing down if Mom decided to go inside to make sure Elle had permission to go. *Please, please God, for once, let Mom just go!*

Mom sighed, shook her head, and put the car in reverse. "Elle, I sure hope you don't get into trouble with your parents over a silly ballgame." She backed down the driveway and turned to look out into the street, but lights from an oncoming car flashed brightly. The Heavens must have granted my wish—Mom surely would concentrate on her driving and forget about the drama inside Elle's house.

"It's f-fine, Mrs. Ketchings," Elle stuttered from the back seat, "they know about the ballgame; I promise it's okay—Mom even wants me to go."

I flashed Elle a look. She darted a look back, but her eyes were on a roller coaster ride. We both knew better than that. Up until the big cooing and rocking scene, it appeared her mom didn't care whether she lived or died, and even now I wondered if it was all for show.

Elle dragged her eyes back to mine and her pain flooded out—all the way to the front seat. She gets that look from time to time, and I don't know what else to call it other than 'worry', it could be fear, or hurt, all I know is she has different looks and this one definitely isn't the happy one.

After three light-years, Mom wheeled into the parking lot. Determined to leave my troubles at the door, I linked an arm through Elle's, and we pushed inside. The crowd was of titanic proportion—I figured there was no way we'd find two seats together, but luckily there were two spots on the first bench. Right. Next. To. The. Cheer. Team. Karma was an evil old biddy that shadows my every move, seeking every opportunity to hurl me into Lexi's world.

"Come on, A.J." Elle yanked me toward the seats. Her worried look was now replaced by a grin and dancing eyes. She totally spazzed me out sometimes. Either she had the uncanny ability to forget whatever troubled her earlier or she was a pro at hiding her feelings. I'm opting for the latter. "They're the best seats in the gym. Forget Lexi and her goons. You can't run and hide all your life."

You do, I silently shouted. I zipped my mouth and followed Elle to the seats.

Lexi saw us coming and whispered something behind her hand to Goon Number 1—or was it Goon Number 2? Whatever, it must have been the funniest joke in the world, according to the way they hee-hawed.

We sat down and I gazed at my classmates all decked out in jeans and tees. Me? I looked like last year's ad campaign for Mary Poppins. Jerking off the plain red vest, I crammed it under my feet. I looked down and saw a big brown splotch splashed across the entire front of my shirt.

Tugging the dreadful vest back over my head, I crossed my arms over my chest. So much for haute couture. On a scale of one to ten, my wardrobe hunkered down around a minus twelve on good days—this wasn't one of them.

Elle jabbed me with her elbow. "Look! The team's lining up. Get ready to cheer for your boyfriend."

I tossed a look toward the cheer team. "Shhh! He's not my boyfriend." I felt the burn ignite my face. If I could wish for a superpower, it would be to disappear at will.

"Tell him that." Elle leaped to her feet along with the other screaming fans as the cheer team fashioned a line for the approaching team. "T-R-O-J-A-N-S. *TROJANS! TROJANS! We're The Best!*"

Too late, I realized I was the only one sitting on our side of the gym, so I jumped up and joined in on the cheer. *"Trojans! Trojans! We're The Best!"*

A quick burst brought Bryant Baker crashing through the paper sign—Captain of the team. He was the captain of my heart, too. Time froze, the din diminished, the gym emptied as I spazzed gaga over his tall frame, hoping against hope he'd pick me out, look my way, and wink.

Didn't happen. Instead, Bryant Baker high-fived Lexi as he ran past; she turned and blew him a kiss—at his back. My hate-monitor sky-rocketed to an all-time high, and on a scale of one to ten, that blown kiss was minus twenty-two thousand.

Three cheers later, the game finally started, and I settled back to cheer Bryant on. Maybe I didn't scream his name every five seconds, but I drooled over his every move–whether he had the ball or not. When he scored, I melted, thinking surely each basket was just for me. After he netted the winning shot, he looked straight at me and gestured 'thumbs-up'. (It's possible he meant that for his brother sitting two rows back.)

"Come on!" Elle pulled me to my feet.

"Where are we going?" I scrambled along behind her.

"To congratulate the team."

Elle didn't let go until we stood outside the locker room with all the other fans–all except Lexi, she was nowhere in sight. I figured she was probably touching up her makeup, or else she was too important to stand around and wait for *anyone*.

Finally, the team drifted out and Bryant brought up the rear.

"Good game, Bryant," Elle said.

I nodded. "Yeah, good game." I couldn't drag my stare from his ice-blue eyes.

Bryant smiled. "Oh hi, Amanda Jo."

My gaze left his eyes to follow his mouth. Like, he knew my name!

Elle leaned in. "It's A.J."

Bryant turned to her. "What?"

The entire time this exchange took place, I stood there, dumbfounded.

"Her name, it's A.J."

have hit a nine for about an hour. When I arrived at the mall to buy the red boots I wanted so badly I could taste them, black was the only color left–that's why my scale meter rarely ever scores above a three.

I decided to go back downstairs and plead with Mom one more time. Leaping off the last step, I came face-to-face with family members arriving in The Magnolia Room. I immediately pulled my 'so sorry for your loss face' and ducked into the Orchid Room. Who chose that name, Magnolia Room, anyway? Dad? Nah. Mom? Nah. Mrs. Dunn? Yeah, it had to be Mrs. Dunn, the be-all, know-all of Funeral Home couture–in her mind, anyway. According to Mrs. Dunn, her way is the *preferred* way, and she's forever rearranging the flowers and the pots to reflect 'better flow'. Who pays attention to flow when they're mourning the dead? Boo-hoo-hoo, we are so sad, but the flow is nice, said nobody ever.

The Orchid Room, which was actually painted lavender, made more sense, even if it was creepy–especially when the coffin was draped in black velvet. The room took on a glow of Count Dracula and his purple-lined cape. Otherwise, it was just as boring as The Magnolia Room.

I flicked the lights on, high sprayed polish over the large desk nearest the door and swiped my cloth across the dark wood. Flowers covered every flat surface and hid most of the dust, but I wiped every surface anyway. I was just finishing up when I caught a glimpse of white-blond hair. No way–who else do I know with that hair color?

I rushed to the door and peeked into the hall just in time to see Lexi and her goons heading toward The Resurrection Room, my least favorite room. When I was nine years old, I learned the definition of that word and refused to go inside because I was scared the bodies would do just that: Resurrect right up out of their coffins and float up to the ceiling–not a good situation for a funeral home. But back to Lexi and her goons–what are they doing here? Up to no good, I bet. Stashing the can of polish and rag into the back of a nearby peace lily, I trailed the trio.

Sure enough, Lexi and her goons bypassed The Magnolia Room and cut a path straight toward old Mrs. Weaver, laid out in The Resurrection Room in all her splendor. Not one visitor, phone call, or next of kin had come forward, and not one person crying to see her go. Mom said it was the saddest thing she'd seen. Could Lexi or her goons be related? I didn't think so. I'd glanced at the obit, but none of the names jumped out at me, not that I really read it, just caught a word here and there after Dad's secretary uploaded the newspaper ad to the big screen. To be honest, the only reason I even look at the big screen in the first place is to chuckle over some of the language–like this one: "Mr. Brown loved gambling, racetracks, and women. He will be missed by all." Now that was funny.

I molded my body to the wall behind the door and watched through the crack as Lexi and her goons walked straight up to Mrs. Weaver's body. What happened next made even me gasp.

Lexi huddled over the coffin, her back to me. I saw her shoulder and arm move like, maybe, she patted Mrs. Weaver's hand. Maybe she was related, after all.

"Did you finish dusting?"

I jumped a good twelve inches off the ground. "Mom, don't do that!"

"Have you finished dusting?" She ground her fists on her hips, her eyes blazing.

"Yeah."

"Good, they are moving the flower arrangements out of the Magnolia room into the Chapel." Mom took a step, then turned, her head cocked to one side. "You did dust the Chapel, right?"

I chewed my lower lip. "You, uh, didn't say anything about the Chapel."

Mom closed her eyes briefly and took a deep breath. "When I tell you to dust the viewing rooms, and you know there's a service tonight, wouldn't you normally also know to dust the Chapel? I declare, Amanda Jo, I do not know where your head is sometimes."

"A.J.," I mumbled under my breath. Where had I stashed the furniture polish? Was it in a pot headed for the Chapel?

Sure enough, I followed Mom out into the hall just in time to see a cart rolling my peace lily down the hall, Johnson's Furniture Polish shining to beat the band, no pun intended. The white rag waved in surrender.

I darted a look at Mom, but her back was to the cart. Now was my chance. I giant-stepped to the peace lily, reached for the items, lost my balance, and fell headlong into a floral spray. I rolled to my feet and quickly plucked white Carnations and Baby's Breath out of my hair, but not quick enough.

"Amanda Jo!" Mom hissed. We tend to hiss a lot inside the funeral parlor. No loud sounds. I think they call it inside voices, or in this case, inside hisses.

Mom concentrated on straightening the flowers on the spray, while I turned to see the white flag wave goodbye as the cart glided toward the front of the Chapel. I stood there, dumbfounded, as Mr. Gray placed my arrangement in a prominent spot near the coffin. I continued to watch Mr. Gray, who can't see beyond the nose on his face without his glasses (and of course, he was forever misplacing them), turn the big plant around, front and center.

The white flag, rag, stuck out like a sore thumb, while the can of furniture polish proudly stood guard at its side. Maybe everyone would think the extras were a huge white bloom and a shiny gold statue of the Virgin Mary. One could hope.

Before I could move, Mom grabbed my elbow.

I winced and clamped my mouth shut to keep from yelping.

"Young lady, Mrs. Dunn said she saw a white cleaning cloth and a can of furniture polish stuck in one of the pots rolling toward the Chapel. You wouldn't happen to know anything about that, would you?" Mom two-stepped me inside the Chapel and down the aisle.

Every eye in that room gyrated from poor old dead-as-a-doorknob, Mr. Reilly, to lock onto me. When I passed by his coffin, I wondered if he hated the stares as much as I.

Mom grabbed the dusting supplies and stuffed them inside her jacket, without missing a beat.

Mrs. Dunn rushed toward us. "Mrs. Ketchings, Mrs. Ketchings! May I have a word with you?"

There was that hissing, again.

Finally, Mom dropped her hold on me and thrust the offending can and cloth into my hands. "Put these in the cleaning closet and go straight to your room." She plastered her face with her fake smile and set off toward Dad's assistant.

I wanted nothing more than to escape, but Mrs. Dunn's next words froze me in my tracks. "Mrs. Weaver's jewelry, it's gone!"

What? I eased over to the sliding wall.

"What do you mean 'it's gone'?" Mom's voice registered full-panic.

"I, myself, inventoried Mrs. Weaver's jewelry—she had on two rings, a watch, and a broach." Mrs. Dunn ticked the items off. "I just now peeked in to straighten the flowers, and there's no jewelry on that body. I'm telling you, I know for a fact, she had on that big diamond cluster ring—why not more than an hour ago; oh, what will we do? Somebody stole poor Mrs. Weaver's jewelry!"

Lexi—she didn't pat Mrs. Weaver's hand. She stole her jewelry!

Chapter V

The Right Side of Wrong

I considered telling Elle about the missing jewelry, but when I played out the scene in my mind, I knew she would freak and drag out the big guns. I could see Elle blasting her way into the lunchroom in a matchy-matchy cowgirl outfit (compliments of her mother, of course), shouting through a megaphone: *You're going down, Grave Robber.*

No, I decided to handle this on my own, without Elle. I would determine when to back off and when to push, no goons, no Elle, just Lexi and me; but if there was such a thing as ghosts and spirits, I could use a little help, Mrs. Weaver, if you're listening. After all, the jewelry DOES belong to you–just stay in the background, though; I don't need to see you.

On Monday, I caught up with Lexi in the cafeteria. "I need to talk to you, alone." I kept walking toward the bathroom, and I truly was shocked to see her enter right behind me.

"You have some nerve..." Her blue eyes narrowed, rigid and icy.

Normally, my gut would churn fear and firecrackers, but I stuck my hand in front of her face as if I were stopping traffic. "Save it—this is serious."

"Better be, if you know what's good for you." She crossed her arms over her chest.

I sucked in a deep breath. Nerves threw me into a coughing fit. When I stopped spurting and hacking, my voice sounded like a foghorn. "I saw you take that jewelry from Mrs. Weaver's body, and you can either hand it over or I'm going to the cops—this is one time you're not getting away with stealing. Can you be more disgusting? Robbing a dead person? Really?" I gasped another breath and waited.

What happened next was the most bizarre thing in the world: Lexi's eyes filled with tears. She cupped one hand over her mouth and silently sobbed, shoulders bobbing up and down like a jackhammer.

Then, the second most bizarre thing in the world happened: my heart broke—for Lexi Lanthrope! The room shrunk three sizes.

All I wanted was to transpose myself anywhere away from this freaking bathroom. "Uh, okay, just so we're clear—you'll give it back, right?" I shoved past Lexi, raking my sweaty palms down the side of my jeans, and butted my shoulder against the hard door.

"She was my Grandmother."

I froze. *"WHAT?"* I jerked around; the door hit me in the butt. "What did you just say?"

Lexi's eyes, motionless on the floor, whispered, "She is, was, my Grandmother." She appeared dead-serious, another pardonable pun.

Still, I was not letting Lying-Lexi fib her way out of this. "You're making that up–everybody knows your parents are doctors." I had never exhibited this much gumption in my entire life, but I also had never been so petrified. My heart galloped like the lead horse in a race.

"I'm adopted." Lexi swiped a glob of snot from her nose.

Yuk, even the great Lexi Lanthrope snots.

If I thought my mouth was dry before, now it felt like a desert during an epic sandstorm, with a parade of camels marching through. On top of that, my stomach knotted in a painful cramp, as the air whooshed out of my lungs. "You're lying." Inside my thumping heart, a tiny butterfly fluttered.

Lexi met my eyes and glared back. "Who lies about something like that? Maybe lie and say you're NOT adopted–never that you are, get a life." She sighed and rolled watery eyes away.

"So you...who? How?" My fleeting thoughts flashed by so fast, I couldn't hang onto any.

Lexi swiped the back of her hand under her nose. "Mrs. Weaver's daughter, Celia, got pregnant with me at sixteen; she gave me up–my parents adopted me when I was two days old."

I fell back against the door. "So, like, your parents, the doctors, they are your adoptive parents, and they adopted you when you were two days old?" I paused to let it gel. "So, like, they just adopted you right after you were born, and no one knows you're adopted?" No matter how many times I said the "A" word, it still wouldn't click; but then again, nobody lies about their birth–not even Lexi, right?

"Some people know." Lexi yanked toilet paper off a roll and blotted her eyes. She blew her nose–a lot; finally, she washed her hands, with soap, and I immediately felt better. Lexi slung the water off her hands and reached for a towel. "Mrs. Weaver never had another thing to do with her daughter after she gave me up. Mom said she wanted to raise me as her granddaughter, but Celia wanted the money, instead; so, Mrs. Weaver disowned her."

Lexi tossed the towel in the garbage and continued. "Celia stayed with Mom and Dad, my adoptive Mom and Dad, until I was born." She met my eyes. "They paid for doctor visits, her food, everything–then gave Celia money to start over someplace else. I've never laid eyes on my birth mother–never wanted to. I guess I should hate her; but the truth is, I feel nothing for her." Lexi's look wasn't so cocky now. One arm hugged her waist, the other hand-screened her mouth, dulling her voice to a rasp.

A cold shiver slid down my spine, like a spider slipping on ice. "You promise this isn't another one of your lies?" She seemed like she was telling the truth, but this was Lexi Lanthrope. Who could believe a word she said?

"Cross my heart, hope to die." Lexi looked up, mascara-tears, once again, coursing down her splotchy face.

"Well, I hope I don't die, the only family I ever wanted to know is lying in your stupid funeral home as we speak, but you know what I mean."

Something still didn't add up. "So why steal the rings?"

Lexi ran the water over a towel and attempted to wash the mascara from her face. "Celia is a Meth addict. I overheard Mom and Dad talking about how many times she has contacted them over the years, and now, apparently, she's heard about Mrs. Weaver's death and wants money for an attorney. I guess she plans to sue the estate." Lexi paused, met my eyes, and held the stare. "Like, if her own mother didn't want Celia to have the jewelry, how could *I* stand around and wait for her to swoop in and take it?"

"Did your parents give her money?"

Lexi's sour look told me more than I needed to know. "No way would they help her now."

"I still don't get it. Why would Celia need to hire an attorney in the first place? Wouldn't she inherit the stuff anyway? She is still her daughter, not a very good one, but blood is thicker than water, right?"

Lexi raised her palms. "Duh. Are you dense? I told you Mrs. Weaver disowned Celia long ago–cut her out of the will, I guess you'd call it; anyway, Celia is one bad dude, and Mrs. Weaver didn't consider her family anymore. It's not like I was there, but from what I pieced together, whatever blood remained between them, was bad."

"Oh yeah, right..."

Lexi's eyes found mine in the mirror. "I am not letting Celia get her grubby hands on anything. Besides, it's not like we're family...Celia and me. She never cared anything about me. All she's interested in is where she can score her next high."

I still wasn't convinced. I ticked off each item on my fingers: "So, like, your adoptive parents are the doctors, and you are really Mrs. Weaver's, err, granddaughter; you thought you'd just beat your real mom stealing Mrs. Weaver's jewelry, right?" I looked back at her in the mirror. "Then how does that make you any better than Celia?"

Lexi flung around. "Don't you dare compare me to that selfish Meth addict, besides the jewelry is all I have left of my Grandmother." Red splotches flooded her cheeks; her brows met in the middle. "Don't you get it, you idiot? My parents broke down and told me about my Grandmother after Celia threatened to tell me, herself. Apparently, she'll try anything, even blackmail."

I guess I could understand Lexi wanting a keepsake to remember her Grandmother by, still... I leaned closer. "I'll keep my mouth shut, for now, but only because I don't know if I believe you or not." I stuck my finger in her face. "If I find out you're lying..."

"Whatever." Lexi shoved past me. "Do whatever you've got to do." She stopped at the door but never looked back. "I'm keeping the jewelry. It's your word against mine. And Jen and Blair will back *me* up."

I watched the door swing shut. Now, this is the Lexi I knew. Still, what would I do in her case? If true, Celia shouldn't get the jewelry, but stealing was stealing. And besides, what guarantee did I have Lexi was telling the truth?

Every time I saw her that day, she seemed different. Quieter. And the creepiest thing was, like, something inside me softened toward her. I'm not saying we would ever be friends or anything, but I didn't feel total hatred toward her, like before. Maybe she doesn't have everything she wanted, after all. Maybe I have the one thing she doesn't have: a real family—not that having two doctors for parents, a big house, and the best clothes money can buy wasn't everything. Look at Elle, though. She has lots of things and she's miserable. Maybe I'm the lucky one.

After lunch on Tuesday, I caught up with Lexi in the hall. "Okay, I've thought it over."

Lexi couldn't look at me for gazing around the hallway to see if anyone saw me talking to her.

"Maybe you're telling the truth, but stealing is wrong. You need to tell your parents and let them decide."

"I thought about that, but if I do, they'll make me give the jewelry back. That is not an option." She ducked her head closer to me, and I stared at what had to be the straightest part in the history of the world, down the center of her white hair, with bangs falling straight to the bridge of her nose. So, when had Lexi cut bangs? Are bangs even in?

I blinked and rushed on. "Mrs. Weaver will be buried tomorrow, and as far as I know, no one has ever claimed the body. Maybe Celia's dead, too."

Lexi darted another look around the hall before continuing, "My parents are paying for the funeral, but they won't have any involvement with the service. Look, the jewelry isn't even worth anything, except to me." She brushed her hair out of her eyes and crammed a long strand behind her ear, but it sprung back.

"Then come clean. Who is left to leave her stuff to? It'll probably wind up going to you, anyway. It's just wrong to steal it." I turned to leave.

"Amanda Jo."

Another one knows my name.

I turned and stared her down. "What?"

"Look, thanks for not ratting me out. You didn't have to keep quiet." Once more, her eyes snaked a look to both sides. "And thanks for not making me feel like trash."

Did Lexi Lanthrope just thank me? What the heck! "Forget it. I've done my part–you need to talk to your parents and see what they think." I started to go, but Lexi laid a hand on my arm. Electricity jolted through my body.

"All right, I will try, but I've got to find the right time." She tried to tuck the chopped strand of hair back behind her ear again. Her eyes never left my face, pleading and begging, like my dog when he wanted a treat.

Chapter 13

Goodbye, C'est La Vie, Adios, and Sayonara

Wednesday morning, I crept downstairs to see if anyone had signed Mrs. Weaver's guest book. The page was empty, so I carefully wrote: Amanda Jo Ketchings. *Rest In Peace, Lexi's Grandmother.*

"There you are."

Dang, with Mom around, I get more exercise than running track—or is my guilty conscious having a field day? "You need to quit sneaking up on me."

"You must have a guilty conscience." Mom said the words out loud, but a soft smile eased the sharp edge of her voice. "I definitely didn't sneak up on you." She raised a large envelope. "You'll never believe what this is."

"What?"

Mom shook the envelope and several shiny objects fell out into her hand. "Mrs. Weaver's jewelry."

"No way!" I peered closer. "Where'd you find it?"

Mom slipped the big diamond ring on her finger. "In our mailbox. I guess whoever took the jewelry came to their senses and returned it. I don't know the motive, but I'm sure glad to have it back." She held her hand out to admire the sparkling stone.

That's so not right, trying on poor old dead Mrs. Weaver's ring while she was lying in the next room, even if she couldn't take it with her. Still, my someday-to-be designer gut screamed 'foul'.

I grabbed Mom's hand and pulled at the glimmering stone. "So, what will happen to the jewelry now?" My mind bounced back to Lexi.

Mom helped me remove the ring from her finger and carefully placed it back into the envelope with the other jewelry. "Well, if no one claims it by tonight, we'll bury Mrs. Weaver wearing it." She walked toward the viewing room and Mrs. Weaver's coffin.

I followed. Maybe she really can take it with her. "That's not fair." I peered over Mom's shoulder. "Surely Mrs. Weaver had family somewhere."

Mom raised the lid of the coffin and pinned the broach on the white collar of the purple silk dress. "Well, technically, a prominent family in town paid for her arrangements, but they don't want any recognition. There's nothing else to be done. The jewelry will be buried with the body."

I glanced at Mrs. Weaver's face and couldn't help but notice a tiny smile playing around the edges of her mouth. Was that there before? Maybe she knew and was proud her granddaughter did the right thing and returned the jewelry. But wait! That didn't sound right–why wouldn't she want her granddaughter to have it? I was so confused.

The next day, I somehow lived through all six periods without a run-in with Lexi. Truth be known, she was probably dodging me as much as I was dodging her. After school, I found myself back in the chapel of the mortuary where someone had put the remainder of the jewelry on Mrs. Weaver's body.

The big diamond ring sparkled as if it were happy to be home. I sat down on a bench in the first row and stared at the casket. I imagined the old lady sitting in a rocking chair in a room filled with violets, floral drapes, and stiff white scarves covering the tables. The lady wore Mrs. Weaver's burial dress and the big diamond ring twinkled brighter than the sunlight that poured through a nearby window. I was so lost in thought I barely heard the front door open.

I jerked back to reality as a woman, decked out in white stretch pants and denim shirt shuffled into the room and made a beeline straight for Mrs. Weaver's coffin.

The woman wore dirty white sneakers with no laces. She was a little underdressed for a service. She didn't stop at the seats but walked front and center to stare at Mrs. Weaver's body.

"May I help you?" Mom strolled down the aisle.

I darted a look at the woman's face: tired eyes, deeply lined mouth, and white-blonde hair hanging dirty and limp. White-blonde hair!

"I'm Celia Weaver."

No way, Jose!

"I've come to say goodbye to my mother."

My mouth stuck in open mode, and I couldn't have closed it again if I tried.

This person was Lexi's birth mother!

Mom stopped in her tracks. "Hold on, I'll get my husband. I'm sure you have questions."

Celia Weaver shook her head. "No, I'm not staying. Just came after my stuff."

Mom joined Celia at the casket, where her hands busily tucked a stray flower back into place. "I'm sure you'll want to stay for the service. It's this evening at seven." She turned to the woman. "I'm so sorry for your loss."

Celia ignored Mom's outstretched hand. "No. I'm not staying for the service. I just want what's mine."

"But surely…"

Celia rummaged in a dirty purse. "Look, I have my birth certificate, my driver's license, a picture of Mom and me when I was younger, a letter she wrote…see, that return address—here in this town, right? That's her handwriting."

Mom touched the woman's arm. "Let's go into the office. I'm sure we can…"

"I just want her jewelry. Then I'll be going."

"No!" The word flung out of my mouth like a paddle ball on a rubber band.

Mom gawked at me as if I'd cannonballed in from outer space. "Amanda Jo, this doesn't concern you."

I navigated the remaining few feet between Mom and me in a Nano-second. "Why should she get the jewelry? She didn't care anything about Mrs. Weaver. Just ask Lexi."

"Amanda Jo!" Mom turned back to Celia. "I'm sorry, Miss Weaver. I have no idea what's got into my daughter; she normally is very polite in these circumstances." She pulled me a few feet away, pinching a chunk out of my arm. "Young lady, this is none of your business—now you go upstairs to your room, right now."

"Ouch, okay, okay!" I lowered my voice. "Please Mom, it *is* my business. I know something you don't. I..."

Mom's eyes narrowed. "Enough." She spun me around and aimed me toward the door. "Go." She pushed my back and sent me stumbling several steps.

I went, but I stomped all the way. Why I was so upset, I wasn't sure. I didn't even like Lexi.

Up in my room, I played music too loud and spent a lot of time on my bed with a pillow crammed over my head. It would serve Mom right if I smothered; and if Mrs. Weaver had a service, I didn't want to hear. If Celia got the jewelry, I didn't want to know. If I was in trouble with Mom, I didn't care one iota.

Of course, Mom couldn't let it go. About ten minutes later, I heard her footsteps coming up the stairs and heading straight toward my room.

She flung open my door. "Amanda Jo, I want to know exactly what made you act up so?"

I hit the volume on my remote. "Nothing. Please go away."

Mom crossed over to my bed. "I'm not leaving until I hear your explanation and turn that racket down." She reached for the remote, but I beat her to it. She sat on the side of my bed.

I muted the sound. Mom probably couldn't work the remote if her life depended on it.

"You can tell me now or you can tell Dad and me together. Either way, I will hear the truth."

I blew out a loud sigh and covered my head with a pillow. After a few seconds, I peeked out. She meant it, she had that 'I'm not leaving this room until you spill your guts' look.

I took a deep breath, felt my chest quiver, but plunged full force ahead. "Mom, you've got to double-dog swear you won't say anything because it's kind of a colossal secret." The sob sprang up from nowhere, swooshed right out of my mouth, fetching a big fat tear with it.

"Amanda Jo!" Mom smoothed my hair from my face. "What is it, baby?"

That did it. The waterworks turned on full force and I did the unthinkable. I fell on Mom and blurted out, "Lexi is adopted, and Mrs. Weaver's her real Grandmother, and that Celia-woman stole from her before, and it's not fair, and now Lexi won't have anything to remember her Grandmother by."

Mom pushed me away and looked me in the face. "Honey, slow down. Who's Lexi?"

"This girl at school who hates my guts, and I-I can't stand her, either. She stole the jewelry from Mrs. Weaver's body, and I was going to tell on her, but she told me Mrs. Weaver is really her Grandmother." I cried the words out between sobs. "I told her if she didn't return the jewelry, I was going to tell." I broke down again and boohooed like a two-year-old who'd lost her favorite Teddy-bear.

Mom held me tight for a few minutes. "Honey, why didn't you tell me? You should have come to me when you saw this girl take the jewelry." Her words were firm, but she still held onto me.

Spent, I sat up and wiped my eyes. There was never a tissue when you needed one. "I know, but, like, I tried to convince Lexi to return the jewelry. I even threatened to go to the Police, but then Lexi told me Mrs. Weaver was her real Grandmother. I-I didn't know what to do, Mommy." What am I–four years old again?

Mom took a deep breath. "Well, I need to tell your father, but for now, go wash your face and calm down." She followed me to the bathroom and handed me a washcloth.

She was really being nice.

Mom leaned against the door jam. "It appears Celia Weaver is the next-of-kin, and there might be nothing we can do but turn the personal effects over to her if she can prove it."

"It's not fair, Mom." The sobs started again, but not as hard as before. "Lexi's adoptive parents even paid for the funeral. Lexi says Celia will just sell the jewelry for Meth."

Mom pulled me close again. "Honey, there's nothing we can do about that. It's not our say. Celia is in with Dad, now. He'll have our attorneys verify everything, of course; but if she is who she says she is–she's next-of-kin."

"What if she's legally disowned?"

Mom looked at me with a peculiar frown. "That's something the attorney would need to prove. But if true, it might change things. Any rate, it's not our concern."

"Is she at least staying for the service?"

Mom shook her head. "No. However, Mrs. Weaver will have a nice service, anyway." She smoothed my hair. "There'll be four or five of us there, and I picked out some old hymns I think Mrs. Weaver would have liked. Also, a very pretty bunch of flowers arrived a little while ago–pink roses. I heard someone out in the hallway, but they didn't come to the chapel. I did see they had signed the book, under your name. It was just one letter–a capital 'L'. Do you think it might have been this Lexi you mentioned?"

I stopped snubbing. "Can I see it?"

"Sure. Maybe you can be the one to give the book to Lexi. It's not jewelry, but it would make a lovely keepsake to help her remember she now has a Guardian Angel watching over her."

Hmmmm…if Lexi gained a Guardian Angel, maybe she would become a nicer person. That must be what they call a 'win-win'.

Chapter 11

Curiosity Killed The Cat…Now It's After ME!

The next day, math class dragged on and on. When I finally hoofed it to my locker, Elle was nowhere in sight, so I headed outside to the car-pool line and begged Mom to drive me by her house. My cell battery was dead so I couldn't call, but I figured Elle would be happy to see me. She always is—*usually.*

"Is it okay with her mother?"

I lied. "Yeah, they're expecting me." Why did I do that? Lie to Mom. It always comes back to bite me.

Mom darted a sideways look at me. "You know I have my hair appointment downtown, but I guess I can swing back by and pick you up in two hours."

Two hours might work, but I preferred to play it by ear. "How about I call you when I need a ride? We're working on a science project, and it could take a while." It was almost true—for sure, we'd talk about boys and one, in particular. Surely there was a scientific explanation for how tingly my insides felt whenever I saw Bryant Baker.

Mom interrupted my thoughts. "I don't like it when you make plans without talking to me, first." Her stern tone informed me this is not the time to argue. "You call me in one hour, you hear?"

I looked out the window so she wouldn't see my eye roll. "Okay." I might not be able to argue, but I sure could give her the loudest sigh in the history of mankind; besides, for crying out loud, I was almost a freshman, and she still treated me like a kindergartner.

"And make sure you charge up that battery when you get there. You do have your charger, right?" She flashed me *that* look. "You know I don't like you being on your own without a fully operational cell phone."

Yeah, right. Like, I didn't have to fight tooth and nail to get one when I turned twelve.

We pulled into Elle's driveway. Mom put the car in park. Was she getting out? She couldn't be getting out.

"Mom, I'll call you, I promise." Jumping out of the car before she could open her door, I flung over my shoulder. "I'm not a baby, you know; and besides, how am I ever going to learn responsibility if you don't ever trust me?"

"Oh, I don't know. Show some responsibility, and maybe I'll learn to trust you."

I glanced toward the house. Wait. Both cars were at home. Why wasn't Mr. Chambers at work? I needed to go inside, or Mom would realize I lied about being invited. Thanks again, Karma! On a scale of one to ten, my luck usually hovered right around zilch.

Slinging my backpack over my shoulder and hoping Mom hadn't noticed it was my old bag, I sped to the front door and jammed the bell. Nothing. After a few seconds, I hit the bell again and shifted the backpack from one shoulder to the other before ringing again. Thank God, Mom had an appointment downtown or she would have sat there in the driveway judging my every move.

Why was no one answering the door? I tilted closer. Wait, was the front door open? I shielded my eyes and scrunched closer. Sure enough, the door bolt rested against the lock plate, and light streamed through the crack. Mustering courage, I pecked on the glass door. Still no answer. What the heck? I yanked open the glass door and flicked the heavy front door open an inch.

"Hello? Anybody home?"

Still no answer. Maybe I should just leave. Yeah, right, and walk three miles home? I nudged the door another minuscule push.

"Hello? Elle? Mrs. Chambers?"

Nothing.

With a harder push, the door swung wide open. I stuck my head inside.

"Mr. Chambers?"

Well, technically, I was already in; so, my feet just followed my head inside. "Hello?"

Nothing.

Was someone talking in the kitchen? Back to stealth mode, I tiptoed through the living room and slunk toward the kitchen, as if I hadn't just yelled "anybody home" at the top of my lungs.

The voices turned out to be on TV.

"Elle, you here?" My voice rang louder than the commercial and by now, my footsteps were way past tiptoeing.

The kitchen was as clean as ever; matter-of-fact, I'd been in this house several times and never was anything out of place, not a cereal bowl, not a pair of shoes, not even a book, or magazine. It was as if no one lived here.

I turned to leave and that's when I saw the basement door standing open. I had never been to the basement. Mr. Chambers' den was down there, but Elle never seemed to want to go down, or at least not when I was around.

A chilling thought crept into my mind. What if someone fell and couldn't get up? I couldn't just ignore that possibility, so I opted for the most logical choice. I pushed the basement door open a little wider and peered down the steps. Lights were on. Maybe Elle's mom was doing laundry and couldn't hear me.

"Elle?" My voice dropped to whispering level.

There was something very spooky about a basement. No matter how fancy it was. On a scale of one to ten, that basement was about a twenty-nine for spook-factor. I turned to go.

"Mmmmm...."

I froze numb in my tracks. My heart floundered around inside my chest like a fish trying to belly-flop its way back to water. Squatting, I snuck a peek through the opening of the wall and banister. Don't let anybody be down there–please, please, please! Shivers scuttled down my spine as I scanned the room.

The furniture definitely was no match for the rest of the house. Not what I'd seen, at least. This couch was huge and covered in black leather, as were the two chairs. A pool table dominated most of the floor space, a brick fireplace covered one whole wall, and a flat-screen TV hung above the mantle with ESPN flashing on the screen–no sound, only picture. On a scale of one to ten, my spook meter skyrocketed.

Mr. Chambers' den–no mistake about it. Not a book, magazine, or glass...WAS THAT A FOOT?

I collapsed to my knees. If not for the handrail, I would have butt-bumped down the steps to the floor. I needed to get out of there! I jack-knifed up and banged my head on the half-wall. One hand instinctively shot up to embrace the lump, as dizziness overpowered me.

Wait, what if somebody really fell and needed my help? Snatching a steadying breath, I seized the banister and crept down, baby-stepping into the large room to better-see if that really was a foot sticking out from behind the couch — or maybe it's a leftover prop from Halloween?

I turned and took three giant steps back up the way I came down. A door slammed, and I froze in mid-move. My mind sent panic signals to my body, and instead of rushing toward the front door, I swiveled and lunged toward the fake leg behind the couch.

My foot squished on something soft, my hand connected with pliable skin, and I tumbled and rolled toward the wall. In its best Spiderman imitation, my body scaled straight up the wall–several feet, in fact, before gravity prevailed.

I fell again, curling into a tiny ball in the corner–still behind the couch, but definitely not alone. In a true out-of-body slow-motion mode, I choked back bile and shook with pure-unadulterated terror, as I forced myself to look at the leg attached to Mrs. Chambers' body. Her eyes were closed; her head cocked at a sickening angle. Was she dead?

Curiosity temporarily replaced fear as my attention darted to my sticky fingers, and I turned my hand over to see BLOOD!

"NO!" I leaped up and flung the slimy mess from my hand. Black spots shadowed my vision; no longer able to stand, I went down, until cruel, bruising hands yanked me, by the hair of my head, back upright.

Chapter 15

Mr. Ketchings, You Already Know Dr. Jekyll–Meet Mr. Hyde

"How did you get in here?" The creepiest voice I'd ever heard grated in my ear. Hot breath scorched my neck, as I coiled one pulse-beat away from a sprint. His grip tightened–literally ripping my hair out by the roots. Pure panic possessed my soul–like a nightmare unleashed.

"*Help me! Please! Somebody help me!*" My eyes rolled back in my head and darkness danced around inside.

"You shouldn't be here."

My knees buckled and I floated toward the darkness. Another quick yank of my hair jerked me back to reality.

"Ow! You're hurting me!" I smacked the air behind my head, hoping to knock the hand loose. "Please let go. I'll leave. I won't tell anybody."

Did Mr. Chambers think I was a burglar? Did he recognize me? Why was he hurting me? "She…Mrs. Chambers is over there! We need to call 911!" I kept trying to look at him, but his grip was so firm even a small movement on my part shot hot fiery needles through my scalp.

After what seemed like hours, Mr. Chambers released my hair, but he didn't relinquish his hold on my wrist–not until he turned to look in the direction of his wife. I sprang for the stairs, but he was lightning quick. He grabbed the same wrist, twisting my arm back behind me, shooting painful darts to my shoulder, causing my legs to buckle.

"You're hurting me." Scalding tears poured down my face. I was no match for his strength.

"Shut up," Jay said.

I would forever think of him as 'Jay' now–no respecting this elder, *this* elder was a monster, and *this* monster had a name–Jay.

With brute force, he half-shoved, half-carried my tormented body to the center of the room.

"Who knows you're here?" He tightened his grip on my arm, but this time, he tugged me upward.

I lurched sideways as blistering, blinding knife-blade spears raged through my distorted shoulder. Just when I thought I couldn't tolerate any more pain, a bone snapped. I howled as a new lava-hot liquid scalded my torso. *"Please don't do this!"* I clawed, scratching my way to my feet–attempting to lessen the torture, even if only a tiny bit. Whatever happened, I could not collapse back to the floor. No way could I allow my body to go down. I had to stay higher than his hand. "Why *are* you doing this?" I blubbered, rising to my tiptoes, seeking relief in any way possible.

When I rose, so did his hand–pushing, grinding already-broken bones to a new level of torment.

"Who knows you're here?" Jay demanded again, this time louder, scarier, his mouth only inches from my ear.

I could smell his anger. "My mom." After a second or two, I added, "And my dad." I shot a glance sideways toward his face. Dark. Mean. Who was this person and what had happened to Mr. Chambers?

"You're not supposed to be down here. This room is off-limits."

I rose higher on my toes. "Please let me go. My arm…I think it's broken. Please…"

No good. He yanked my arm higher.

"Stop! Please! I'm sorry." Harsh fear and harsher pain spilled fresh tears. "I'll go. Just let me go."

"You're not going anywhere, missy."

Pain wracked my entire body. "Let me go, please. And where's Elle? I told her I was coming. Mom's upstairs–she'll be down here any second. Dad, too. We're going shopping and out to eat and to a movie…*OH!*"

"Shut up!" Jay dragged me to one of the chairs and slammed me into it. "Stay there."

The pain from the instant release sent prickling needles stabbing hard and deep from my shoulder to my fingertips–so-much-so, the room shot black, and vomit filled my mouth. This time, the bile spewed out. I bent over and violently regurgitated the pain he'd enforced all over his designer shoes. "PLEASE HELP ME!"

Jay backhanded me across the face, sending me careening back to the floor. "Shut up or you'll really be sorry!"

Silver stars burst into icicles, stabbing through my head as I grabbed my face and balled up. As scared as I was of dying here in this creepy basement, I was even more scared of the pain. I craved release. Part of me wanted to trade my next breath for no more pain. Right then, right there, in that foreign basement, eyes shut tight to prevent staring into the face of a monster, death beckoned. No more fear, no more pain—just float to the ceiling and never look back. I recognized death.

STOP! I shook the mist from my head and once the initial burst of pain subsided, determination poured in. There was no Calvary riding to my rescue. It was up to me whether I live or die.

What were Mom's final words when she dropped me off? *I* need to be responsible.

A muffled sob escaped my bruised lips as I pulled myself straight up into a sitting position on the floor. I pushed past the pain. I forced my head to grab onto a thought that teased from some deep recess inside my brain: Jay was the one who beat Elle, not Mrs. Chambers.

I stole a glance toward Mrs. Chambers. Filling my lungs with sweet oxygen caused a crazy feeling of euphoria. Chains fell from my body. I forced myself to take another deep breath and shoved the pain deeper.

My eyes crawled back to Jay. He looked different: weird, confused, and maybe insane. Did he even know me? Drawing another intense breath, I cleared my throat.

"I'm A.J...Amanda Jo–don't you recognize me?" My eyes darted from his bowed figure toward the door in the opposite direction. Is that another way outside? Maybe I could make a run for it.

Bump.

I jerked my head toward the other end of the basement. Another door! Was someone behind that door?

"Help me!" I kicked hard at Jay's leg.

For a split-second, he tottered and went down on one knee.

I took advantage of the distraction and lunged toward the stairs.

Jay was soon on top of me, clutching my left ankle and yanking until I whacked the floor.

I fought, twisting, turning, and kicking with my right foot. The crack was loud, but several seconds passed before the hot streak of liquid pain shot through my ankle. *"Oooooowwwww! You broke my foot!"*

Jay scrambled to his feet, hauling me with him, my broken arm cradled tightly against my chest, my broken foot dangling painfully.

"You think someone is coming to help you?" His face screwed into an ugly grin. "Good idea. Let's go see what's behind door number two." He dragged me across the room, hopping and screaming.

Halfway across the room, I broke free and made a crazy hopping dash around the pool table—as if I could possibly out-hop him. He yanked me backward by my hair, again, crooked an arm around my neck, and squeezed tight.

"Please, please…" I clawed at his face, clawed at his eyes, clawed for breath until white spots invaded my eyes. My head bobbed back. My knees sagged.

I recognized the same promise of release. There in the distance, soothing light lurked right beyond my grasp. It drew me. I wanted to go.

Jay shook me. "Wake up! When are you going to realize there's no way out?"

A lightening sharp pain jabbed at my temple, joined by a renewed pain in my foot. That's when it hit me: If he has his way, I would truly die. I would never live to be eighteen and never get that blue Mustang. My cold dead body would be just another DP lying in a coffin in the Chapel, just like poor old Mrs. Weaver. I could even see Mom standing over me, crying and saying, "She really was a screw-up, but she was my baby." The played-out scenario warmed my hurting heart, and for a few seconds, I reveled in the pity party.

Jay flung open 'door number two', and my self-pity vanished.

Chapter 16

Nightmare On Elle's Street

Elle lay sprawled on the floor of the closet, her legs and arms pointing in different directions.

A sour taste erupted in my mouth; I swallowed quickly and felt the burn. "Elle!"

My twists and jerks couldn't break me loose; instead, Jay thrust me inside and slammed the door. As I fell to the floor, the lock clicked, and immediately, the closet morphed into a petrifying dungeon.

I splayed my fingers in front of my face but could see nothing–not even a hint of movement. Was Elle dead? *Oh God, help me help Elle!* Horror seized me. Flinging myself on the door, I hammered the heavy surface with my good fist. "Let me out of here! Please!"

Even the slightest movement heightened the pain level in my shoulder, producing a debilitating stab ricocheting down my arm and across my neck. I cradled my arm across my chest and plummeted to the floor, rocking and crying. *Why God? Why me?* Why Elle and Mrs. Chambers? Why let Jay win–he was the true monster, why let him win?

Seconds, maybe minutes, passed before I realized I'd wafted back down the dead-end street to defeat. Either I construct a plan to get out of this place, or all three of us were good as gone.

A Bible verse from my childhood flooded back. When I was ten years old, the scariest basement in the world was my own. In order to get to Mom's canned foods, I had to walk past the embalming room on my way to our locked, unfinished basement. Sure enough, every time Mom needed canned tomato juice, corn, or pickled okra, she sent me down to fetch it. There was no getting out of it.

I repeated the Bible verse over and over in my mind. It helped then, maybe it would help now. I closed my eyes and willed myself to concentrate. *What time I am afraid, I will trust in thee. What time I am afraid, I will trust in thee.*

Gaining courage, I scrambled to my knees and rammed an ear to the door. Outside, Jay scuffled around the room, pushing or pulling something across the wood floor. Furniture? Mrs. Chambers' body?

"Help me. Somebody, help me!" I beat the door again, thrusting a throb through my good arm. What a time for my cell battery to go down—the one time I needed my phone.

I kneeled back toward where I'd last seen Elle and patted the floor to locate her wrist. She had to be alive. Please God, let her be alive. She moaned before...right? I blocked my mind to outside noise, as my heart hammered on at full speed.

No pulse. I shifted my fingers and waited. I held my breath. Was that…could that be…? Yes! A tiny beat, then another. Thank God! She's alive!

I couldn't remove my fingers from Elle's wrist–afraid if I turned loose, she would too. As long as I felt that tiny pulse, I wasn't alone–my friend was with me in this death trap.

"You can let go, now."

I jerked my hand from Elle's wrist as if she suddenly became poker-hot. "You're alive!"

"Shhhh! Don't let him know I'm conscious, or he'll come to finish the job."

I lowered my voice. "What's going on? And your mom…she's really hurt."

She stiffened beside me. "Is she…do you know if she's alive?" Her voice broke. "Please let her be alive!"

I wrapped my arm around her thin shoulders and whispered in the vicinity of her ear. "I don't know. She was horribly still, but maybe she's acting, too."

I winced as a flash of the all-familiar white-hot pain knifed through my ankle. Shifting my leg, I carefully stretched it out and took another deep breath. "We've got to get out of here."

Elle's voice sounded strong. "Don't let him know I'm awake. We just need to stay safe for a few minutes longer–maybe you need to bang on the door some more."

"Yeah, like that's going to help us." Still, I gave the door a hefty kick with my good foot. "Let me out of here!" Turning back to Elle, I whispered. "Tell me again how

we're going to get out of here–short of a miracle from God."
My mind flew to my ever-present scale of one to ten, but
the fleeting thought escaped me.

She moved her hand down my arm until she
grasped my hand and shoved something hard in it–*her cell
phone.*

I choked back a sob. "Call 911!"

"I already did."

For the first time in a long, painful time, a glimmer
of hope oozed through my heart, but it quickly faded.

"Do you smell something?"

"No...wait, maybe." I sniffed toward the door.
"Yeah. What is it?"

"Something burning?"

"Like, fire?" The hair on the back of my neck sent a
shiver down my spine.

Elle sniffed. "Something's not right. Is the house on
fire?"

"Please, no." I touched the door. "I can definitely
feel the heat. OH MY GOSH, we're going to die in this
freakin' closet!"

"We gotta get out," Elle screamed; no longer
whispering.

"Elle, it's getting hot in here. What are we going to
do?"

Elle poked me in the arm. "Here, I was going to use
this if Dad came back."

"What is it?" I groped for her hand. A screwdriver!
"Gimme."

"Can you break the lock with it?"

"I can try." I wiped my hand across the door until I located the lock. The metal definitely was warm when I touched it, but I used my fingers to locate the door frame enough to jam the long blade inside. I wedged it back and forth.

"Try hitting the end of the screwdriver. I read somewhere you could break the lock or pop it out of the door frame. Maybe you can do that."

"Like that's ever going to happen." However, I followed her instructions and braced the screwdriver with my sore arm. I butted the end of the rubber handle with my good hand. The quick jab jiggled my stinging arm and shoulder and the screwdriver popped out of my hand and clanged to the floor. Groping the floor, my hand finally closed over the rubber handle.

"Did you find it?"

I nodded as if she could see. "Yes."

"Hurry! Try again. We must get out of here." She experienced a coughing fit that rocked her frail body so hard I sensed the intensity.

I fingered the metal lock–which was quite a bit hotter than before– and located the deadbolt. Sweat beaded my forehead, my shirt hung damp; gagging and coughing, I forced myself to stay calm.

I wedged the blade of the screwdriver back against the lock and tapped gently, hearing the ping of metal on metal. Working the blade a few times to position it against the lock, I gave the rubber end one light tap. Mustering guts and grit from a force other than myself–that's the only way to describe it–I wielded one gigantic blow.

Whoosh! The door sprang open.

I squinted into the light and bellowed a gut-wrenching scream of sheer terror.

Chapter 17

Drip: Water Faucet, My Nose, Melting Icicles, An I.V.

('E,' All Of The Above)

The face of the man staring back at me came dressed in a uniform–*of a policeman*. If they hadn't arrived on time, Jay would have escaped; and Mrs. Chambers, Elle, and I would have burned up in the fire.

A grueling hour and a half after our rescue, I lay stretched out in a hospital bed, examined by a doctor I didn't know, grilled by an officer I'd never seen before, and kissed continuously by Dad and Mom. I'd never been so happy in my entire life. On a scale of one to ten, that moment was a terrific two thousand.

I reeked of smoke, but apparently, a bath wasn't critical to my health. My cracked ribs sported several layers of white tape that discouraged deep breathing–not that I wanted to breathe deeply. The smoke smell, combined with my own sweat, made puffs through my nose, cupped by my good hand, seem like the way to go.

The super-cute ER doctor had stitched up my left thigh–a cut I didn't even realize I had; but when I saw the ugly gash sporting twelve stitches, that spot throbbed right along with my shoulder and ankle. A couple more stitches went into my left eyebrow where I'd smacked the floor at some point during the great-American 'hop away' around the pool table.

Mom was forever misting up when she looked at me, so I figured I must look pathetic with the white bandage covering the top left side of my forehead, a ginormous bandage on my right shoulder, and my right arm in a sling–an ugly blue sling that clashed with my hair, I might add.

My broken ankle was the worst, though. No way could I get comfortable. Every time I looked at the puffy blue skin that protruded over the temporary splint, I wanted to cry. Tomorrow, I would be fitted for a cast, which would make the end of my school year tank almost as bad as the beginning.

The best part about this whole ordeal was the pain medication dripping through an IV stuck in my arm. It was ordered to make "breathing bearable and the pain tolerable." The verdict was still out on that, but dull pain is better than sharp pain, and after my broken shoulder and ankle, I should know. Of course, I will probably give Grandma a run for her money on being able to predict the weather.

"Are you sure you're okay?" Mom asked for the umpteenth time.

"Yes. I just want to go home." I noticed my three broken fingernails for the first time. Aw, Man!

Dad cleared his throat. "You have to stay the night." He looked twenty years older than he had this morning.

"Why? I'm fine. It's Elle that's hurt." I searched his face. Was there something he wasn't telling me? "I'm okay, right?"

"Yes, you're going to be fine." Mom hugged me tightly.

"Yeah, well, maybe you might want to go a little easy on the hugs, Mom." My ribs reminded me of my fiasco in the basement with a monster. My breath caught in my chest, forcing more tears. "Mom, is Elle really okay? And Mrs. Chambers, she's still alive, right?"

Dad raked his hand through his hair. Dark shadows circled his eyes. "Honey, we're telling you the truth. The three of you inhaled quite a bit of smoke, and the hospital wants to keep you tonight for observation. Plus, you've got to get a permanent cast tomorrow on that ankle. Elle and her mother weren't as lucky as you—if you call what happened luck."

"O' lucky me." I attempted a grin but gave up when a new pain paralyzed my face. Still, I could be alive at home, just as easy.

Dad brushed my hair away from the stitches. "You know Elle is in pretty bad shape, but she'll heal. Her injuries are worse than yours, and it will take time. And Mrs. Chambers, Amy, well, she'll be in ICU for some time, but the last report said she came through surgery, and that, in itself, was a miracle. Every minute she's alive is a miracle. Let's be thankful for that." He pulled the sheet over my arm, but not before I saw the tears filling his eyes.

"It's my fault, Dad." My lips turned inside out as a loud sob escaped from deep inside.

Dad stopped with the covers to look me in the eye. "What's your fault, honey?"

"I'm such a screw-up. I lied about them expecting me." I shot a quick look at Mom.

Mom's eyes blinked once...twice, like some crazy Morse code. "They weren't expecting you?"

I snuck another look at her face. "No, I lied to you and see what it got me?" Tears fell out of my eyes. I wrapped one arm around my torso to counter the knife-sharp pains stabbing my insides. "I almost got killed. Elle and her mom, too." I huffed and puffed to hold back the sobs. My ribs couldn't take the jerking, and I expelled what little breath I'd held. "Ahhhhhh..." I tried to sit up, clutching my side.

Mom gently forced me back on the pillow. "Hush honey, just lie still and try to relax. You can't be doing all this moving around with broken ribs. Hush...let your breathing slow down."

"Mom, you know it's true." I clenched my teeth. "If only..."

Mom kissed my forehead. "Listen to me, you are not to blame. No, you shouldn't have lied, but what if you hadn't gone over there? What if..."

My eyes crawled to join hers and tears poured down my face again. "If I hadn't gone, it would be just like all the other times. Elle had bruises all over her body. I saw them, but when I asked her, she pretended like she fell...or hit her arm...or something. She covered for him." I shut my eyes hard–the only part of me that didn't hurt. "Why? Why did she protect him? Why didn't she tell someone?"

Dad gently folded his big arms around me, and I snuggled down in the safe haven. "We don't know, honey. We may never know how long the beatings have gone on. That might explain how Amy, Mrs. Chambers, would keep to herself some of the time...why we wouldn't see her for long stretches of time." He shook his head. "If anyone is to blame, it's me. I'm responsible for bringing that monster into our lives, but I swear I didn't know." His voice broke; he buried his head in my hair and sobbed.

I'd never heard my dad cry before, and I hope I don't ever again. "Dad." I patted his head awkwardly. "It's not your fault. Who knew Jay was a monster? I mean, something was definitely going on there, but to me, every indication pointed to Mrs. Chambers. Not even Elle would talk about it, though. I tried to get her to open up to me, but she pretended everything was okay." My chest felt like a big rock landed square in the middle of it, and I so wanted to take in a lungful of air so bad.

Mom turned toward the window. I knew she didn't want us to see her crying.

"Both of you, it will be okay." I reached a hand out for Mom. "Mom? Really, it will be okay."

Mom turned, grabbed my hand, and clutched it against her face. I saw the tears she tried to hide. "You could have died in that burning house ..."

"But I didn't."

Mom nodded but wouldn't let go of my hand.

"And he...Jay...he's really dead?"

Snatches of conversation surrounding my rescue floated in and out of my mind. I remember seeing shooting flames when our prison door popped open. And somewhere in the back of my mind, I know the fire department sprayed the entire house down with yards and yards of black hoses. Beyond that, things get hazy. As I was loaded into an ambulance, I do remember hearing someone scream for the firemen to get Elle out, too. I'm pretty sure that someone was me.

My head hurt from trying to sort it all out, but some part of me knew Jay was dead. Faint images of a shape draped in black moved through the cobwebs of my brain. If Mrs. Chambers and Elle were here in this hospital, then it had to be Jay, right?

When Dad finally lifted his head, he still had tears running down his face, and all I could think of was Dad...crying! On a scale of one to ten, that moment was a minus ten. A knot tightened in my chest reminding me of the blinding pain when my foot broke–and I thought that hurt! This hurt was a different kind–one I blamed myself for causing. I couldn't make it go away, and I couldn't take it back. Clutching a pillow against my chest, as the therapist taught me to do when I needed to cough, I joined my family in tears, until no more tears would come.

Mom finally wiped her eyes and turned to me. "Hush, honey. It's going to be alright." I buried my face in her shoulder. She smelled like, well, Mom–familiar and safe.

Dad awkwardly patted my back and uttered sounds that were so unlike any I'd heard before. He also cleared his throat, a lot. They both stayed all night with me in the hospital. Dad stretched out on a rollaway bed, and Mom curled up tight against my back in the narrow bed.

Normally, I'd want my space, but this was one time I couldn't be alone. I kept reminding myself Jay was dead, but a part of me was afraid he'd sneak into my hospital room to finish the job.

Poor Elle! If I was scared, how terrified was she? Or maybe she was finally free for the first time in years. Why had she not confided in me, her best friend? And how could I have missed the signs that her father was the one who inflicted the pain? Jay worked at Dad's Funeral Home, they'd eaten at our house, and I had even liked him better than Mrs. Chambers. Why hadn't we all realized what was going on right under our noses?

Mom rubbed my back. "Shhhh….it's okay, Amanda Jo. Just relax, honey. Nothing or no one will ever hurt you like that again, not if I can help it."

I attempted to roll over to gaze into Mom's face. "It was Elle's dad who caused all those bruises. How could he do it, why would he do it?"

Dad rose on one elbow. "We don't know what's been going on in that family, honey. Best not try to figure it out at this point. You need to rest. You'll have a rough time ahead supporting Elle when the truth comes out. You need to sleep, now."

I lay back down. "Can we leave the light on?"

Chapter 18

King Kong Was Only A Monkey On Steroids

On a scale of one to ten, physical therapy sucked a major ten. How many times does one person need to walk the length of a room on crutches? I get it: the crutches replace my broken right ankle; no sir, I won't put any weight on that foot; yes sir, I understand how important it is to let the bones heal.

The doctor hadn't released me to go back to school yet, which meant I could go to therapy every day, five days a week. Mom sat in the waiting room while I did my exercises, then we'd take the elevator upstairs to see Elle.

Elle's body might be healing, but her head still had a long way to go. It had already been a week since that horrible day; one week since Elle had been admitted into the hospital; one week of lying in a bed, being poked and prodded, rolled from side-to-side. No one mentioned when she might go home, but where exactly would she go? Her mom lay two floors up in a coma and her monster of a dad was dead. I'm not sure exactly how Elle could be anywhere but here.

Elle had two broken legs, a ruptured spleen, a broken shoulder, wrist, and all five fingers on her left hand, a concussion, and stitches over sixty percent of her body. She could have easily played the starring role in a horror movie with her head shaved on the left side, making her look like a punk rocker. The purple bruises around her eyes only added to the overall picture. She tried to act as if it was nothing, but I knew for a fact she kept a small mirror under the sheet. Heck, she was alive. I thought she never looked better.

A wave of shame slammed my face. Here I was stressing over physical therapy and Elle wouldn't be well enough to *begin* physical therapy for weeks. On a scale of one to ten, Elle was probably hovering around forty below–health-wise, anyway.

I tossed my physical therapy ball in the air. I'm supposed to squeeze the ball to strengthen my hands and fingers, I guess. "So, I'll call you every day with your homework assignments, and we'll make sure you finish ninth grade. Don't stress over school."

Elle stared out the window, but the heavy look on her face told me she wasn't worried about school. "My dad…I can't believe he's really dead."

I swallowed. Here's the part I've been dreading. "I'm sorry, Elle, but why didn't you tell someone?"

She ignored my question. "Did he…did the police shoot him?"

"I-I don't know. I didn't ask." I missed the ball and watched it roll under her bed. I looked back at Elle's face. "I heard some shots before they got us out–like, there were a bunch of shots. Didn't you hear them?" This was the first time we'd talked about that day, and suddenly, I had lots of questions.

Elle's eyes met mine; she looked away and nodded.

"Have you talked to the police much?"

"Twice. They're coming back today." She rubbed her hand over some stitches that held her arm together. "I just want to see my mom, but they won't let me." She turned her head back toward the window. "My Aunt Gayle is coming today from New York. I guess she's the only family Mom and I have now. It'll be good to see her, maybe she can tell me how Mom really is."

I had no words, so I just stared out the same window.

After a few minutes of silence, Elle continued. "She lives in New York, for crying out loud. I mean, she has a job and everything." She shook her head. "Doesn't add up–and no one's telling me anything." She rolled her head back to me. "A.J., you've got to help me. You've got to find out about my mom." Her chest heaved up and down as her breathing altered to gasps, throwing the nearest machine into action, honking like a flock of geese.

Before I could speak, the door banged open and a nurse rushed in. She was a dead-ringer for Hitler, without the mustache. Well, truth be told, she did have a mustache, just not as dark. The nurse marched straight up to the machine and punched a button.

"Do we need anything in here? Are we doing okay?" She shot a look in my direction that said 'what have you done now'?

Elle nodded. "I'm fine. I just want to see Mom. Can you take me to see her?" Her face twisted into a grimace that indicated pain, a lot of pain, not only from her body.

The nurse's creases morphed into what might pass for a smile. She smoothed those ever-loving covers around Elle, again. "Liebchen, as soon as you're able to make the journey, we'll wheel you up to see your mom. Your mom, she's still in a coma, but there's nothing to be alarmed about." She pointed an index finger at Elle. "Right now, young lady, you're the one that concerns me. You need to take some liquids–if you don't get some nourishment into you, we'll have to start a feeding tube, and you don't want that, now do you?" The nurse waggled her head from side-to-side.

"No, she doesn't." My head followed suit, side to side. "She'd love a strawberry shake." I silently pleaded with Elle.

"Yes." Elle's eyes burned a hole in mine. "I'd love a strawberry shake."

Nurse Hitler smiled. "That's just peachy. I'll call down and get them to send one up." She bustled out the door.

Bustled. I had never used that word before in my entire life, but that's the only way to describe that exit. About thirty minutes later, after I'd finished the remaining three-fourths of Elle's strawberry shake so she wouldn't get a feeding tube, Mom poked her head into the room.

"There's my girls."

Elle's gaze turned back to the window.

I reached for my crutches and turned to Mom. "So, where'd you go?"

Mom twisted the wand on the blinds to let more sunlight pour in. "Why? What did I miss?"

"Elle's aunt is coming today." I turned back to Elle. "What's her name again?"

"Gayle." Elle wouldn't look at me.

"Her Aunt Gayle is coming to stay with her, did you know about that?"

Mom walked to the bed, but she didn't look at Elle or me. "I did." She picked at an invisible object on the covers. "Her flight arrives at two. Your dad is picking her up." She patted the sheet around Elle's body. What was up with this sheet thing? It seemed like every adult on the planet needed to straighten Elle's sheet.

Mom looked my way without making eye contact. "You about ready to go? We are stopping by the school to get your books, and it's back to school for you Monday." She looked like she'd just bit into a lemon. Shooting a glance in Elle's direction, she quickly added, "And you're not far behind her, honey."

Elle didn't make a sound.

"Well, see you tomorrow, Elle." I hopped to scotch myself on my good foot and stuck the crutches under my arms. "I'll bring your books with me. Tell me your combination, again."

"I'll text it to you." She grabbed her cell phone—the Cell Phone that saved our lives. "Make sure you bring my lit book, and please come back soon." Her mouth quivered. She blinked several times.

I was right. Elle wasn't out of the jungle, yet; and big, hairy Gorillas lurked behind every tree.

Chapter 19

BB and The Screamer

My first day back to school was strange. By the end of the day, the entire student body told me how glad they were I was going to be okay. All of them asked about Elle. Everyone except Lexi, that is. Her eyes caught mine a time or two and something I didn't recognize poured out. She never said a word, but her eyes spoke volumes. Compassion? Sympathy?

Mom eased the car up to the main entrance of the funeral home, and I hobbled out. "I'll take the elevator," I yelled over my shoulder. The three steps up to the porch almost killed me; imagine what ten or fifteen steps would do. I stopped and took a breath. *This sucks big time. What did I ever do to Elle's dad to deserve a broken foot? But then, what did Elle do, period? Get born?*

"You need help?" Mom asked all bent over in the back seat, her backside bobbing, turquoise stretch pants expanded to the limit. She straightened up. "I'll carry up your books."

Good old Mom. And Dad, for that matter. "Leave Elle's books in the car. We need to take them to her next time." One, two, swing—six weeks will never get here soon enough. I turned the doorknob and used the tip of one crutch to shove the door open. A loud angry voice blared, jerking me to a stop.

"I told you I don't know where my brother is! What part of that can't you understand?" The voice drifted from the offices in the back.

I 'one, two, swung' into the parlor and peered around the stairway to see who was doing all the yelling. A woman with spiked yellow hair stood outside Mrs. Dunn's office. She wore a matching yellow pantsuit. She looked like A Big Yellow Bird Perched on Stilts. I melted into the wall to listen.

Mrs. Dunn's voice pitched calm and low. "Mrs. Andrews, I'm not trying to upset you."

I leaned closer.

"It's just we've had the body for over two weeks and, well, we need to make some sort of decision of what to do with, err, him, err, your father."

I could almost *hear* the smile on Mrs. Dunn's face. She always smiled, even when people around her bawled. That must be what was meant by putting your best face forward.

"Won't you please come in and sit down?" Mrs. Dunn continued. "I'm sure we can find a solution."

"Look, lady," Miss Yellow Bird squawked. "I don't know what else there is to talk about. You say the state says no cremation until all next of kin are notified. I'm telling you, I haven't spoken to my brother in ten years. He could be dead, too, for all I know."

I tried to ignore the throbbing in my ankle as I listened to the long silence, then Mrs. Dunn's asked, "Is there someone else you can call? Another family member who might know where your brother is?"

"No one."

Another silence, then I heard sobbing. I looked around the corner to see Miss Yellow Bird blowing her nose. "You don't understand. He's my father. I want this over." Another big honking nose blow. "I need closure."

Mrs. Dunn turned on the charm. "I *do* understand, but the funeral home cannot keep the body in the freezer indefinitely."

"The body?" Again, the yelling. "He's not just a body. It's my father!"

I peeked from my hiding place once more to see Miss Yellow Bird posed for attack.

"You people might think this is just another day at the funeral home, but this is my father we're talking about."

"Yes, honey, I understand that." Mrs. Dunn sounded like she was wearing down. "But again, we can keep, err, things as they are for only a few more days." Another one of those long pauses. "Oh, here. This may be your solution: a long-term storage facility in Indiana. It's the closest one I'm aware of."

"Ship my daddy to Indiana?"

I leaned more into my crutch to ease my aching ankle as I poked my head out to see.

Miss Yellow Bird thrust her hands on her hips and bent toward Mrs. Dunn's office as if she was going to take flight. "You've got to be kidding me! My daddy ain't never been to Indiana in his life. Besides, they're our arch-rivals in basketball, and Daddy took his basketball seriously. There's no way I'm sending him to Indiana...especially during playoffs."

Mrs. Dunn's voice dripped with sugar. "*O-kayyyyy*, but it may be your only choice, hon."

Dang, she was good. Dad needed to give her a raise.

PING. Mom walked out of the elevator. "There you are. I thought surely you'd fallen down the elevator shaft."

"Shhh!" I tilted my head toward Mrs. Dunn's office. "They're arguing over a stiff."

"Amanda Jo! I've told you to show respect for the dea..."

"Now YOU look here, *HON!*" Miss YB sounded truly mad now. "I don't know where you get off, but you don't decide what my only choice is. I'll be back."

I could hear SLAP-SLAP of sandals smacking the carpet as Miss YB headed straight for my hiding place.

I motioned for Mom to skedaddle, and I tucked back behind the staircase, hugging the wallpaper. I closed my eyes as if that would make me invisible.

"The very nerve of that woman," Miss YB muttered, as she click-clacked by. "I'll show her who's boss. She wants Ralph's signature? I'll give her Ralph's signature. There's more than one way to skin a cat. I'll take care of my poor daddy, and then I'll never step foot inside this place again!" The door slammed shut.

I breathed a sigh of relief. "Man, she's hot."

Mom poked her head out. "Is that poor Mr. Ramsey's family?"

"Not sure, but Mrs. Dunn has all the poop."

"Amanda Jo! Watch your mouth or I'll wash it out with soap. Even if you *do* have a broken shoulder blade and ankle, you're not going to get away with using bad language."

"For saying 'poop'? I thought that would be better than the other word. Jeez."

"And no more 'jeez', either. It's not appropriate."

Her eyes looked as if she meant it. So much for being happy I didn't die. That didn't last long.

Mom headed toward Mrs. Dunn's office.

"I'm out of here." I 'one, two, swung' my broken ankle toward the elevator. When I got to my room, I threw the hateful crutches on the floor and slid onto my bed, propping my foot on a pillow. I punched my iPod buds in my ears with my one good hand. That's when I heard the granddaddy of all screams.

Chapter 10

The Theory of Related-tivity

"Cross my heart, hope to...well, you know." I couldn't shake the shivers I got every time I thought of how Elle and I dodged death in that basement. "Cross my heart and hope to spit."

Elle's bandages, stitches, and casts covered seventy percent of her body. Anyway, she felt good enough to laugh about Yellow Bird and Mrs. Dunn. "So, what caused the scream? Did they cremate the wrong body or something?"

"Well, almost." I flipped channels on her TV.

"Tell me," Elle said. "I need to laugh. I think I can still laugh."

I settled on music videos. "Well, like I said, just as I arrived back to my room I heard this horrendous scream from downstairs–and we're not talking about a polite little exclamation. We're talking about the biggest horrendous, scary Halloween-bloodbath-freakin' gory scene you can imagine, scream, times four." I sucked in a long bellyful of air before continuing. "I jerked my earphones out and held my breath. I mean like, literally held my breath. Dude, we're talking about a ghastly scream, even for a funeral home."

"Okay, I got it. It was a horrible scream. Then what?" Her eyes were big as sand dollars.

"I yelled for Mom, but she didn't answer. So, I pulled myself out of bed and hobbled back down to the elevator."

"And?" She hadn't moved an inch.

"I heard this man shouting at someone, sounded like it came from Parlor B, so I crept closer to see what was going on. Appears that he and his wife were there to view the body, which turned out NOT to be his father, I guess." I looked back at the TV.

She blew out her breath, clutching her side. "So, who was it?"

"What?"

She blew out another mouthful of air. "The body, you dork. Who was it?"

"Oh, I didn't stick around to find out." I glanced back at the TV where Jared Kole's new video was playing.

"You mean you just left? Like, without finding out where the real body was? It could be in the freezer, heading for cremation." She laughed, grabbing her side, again. "Oh, wouldn't that be awful? Funny, but awful."

"Guess so." I was bored with all the funeral home talk. I totally needed to buy that new CD.

The sheet fell off her arm, and I couldn't help notice how thin it was. I quickly looked away. "I don't know...what am I the identificator or something?"

She laughed. "There's no such word as 'identificator'."

"Should be. Anyhow, I guess Dad contacted the other funeral home and told them they sent the wrong body." I turned back to the TV, but no more Jared Kole. "Anyway, I guess they got it worked out, but not one second too soon–our body was scheduled for cremation this evening. Funny, huh?"

She rolled her eyes again, "I thought you didn't know about the body."

"I guess I forgot until now."

"That would have been horrible–if they'd cremated the wrong body; I mean, like, there's no going back, huh?" Her eyes softened, like the new Elle. "Hey, did I tell you I got out of this room for a while today? Pretty pathetic, huh? Breaking News: Nelly Belle Chambers rolled down the hall today." Her eyes flew to mine. She clamped her good hand over her mouth. "Ugh! Forget I said that–never call me that and swear you won't tell a soul!"

"What? Nelly Belle?" I asked, innocently. "Nelly Belle, Elle sitting in a tree..." I guffawed.

"HE called me that, sometimes, when he...when he..." She broke off with a sob and turned back toward the window.

"You've got to find out what happened to the real body," Elle insisted. "Like, is it there or not?"

"It will be soon. Mom said this body was from Albuquerque, but I don't know the details, only they'd shipped the wrong stiff. It was supposed to be the Father of this guy who came for the viewing."

"But wasn't."

I nodded. "But wasn't." The video ended and I turned back to Elle. "So, anyway, this guy's wife screamed and fainted–went down like a puppet on a broken string. Weird, huh? Fainting over a corpse. Like bodies don't ever get mixed up." My hair chose that moment to bug me; I yanked off my scrunchie and re-strung my ponytail. "When do you get to wash your hair?"

"Nobody's said… my head still hurts–mostly from the stitches over here, not like the throbbing before." Her eyes glazed over for a few seconds like a bad memory threatened to invade her thoughts.

I shuddered, reliving those same memories, and plunged ahead. "Look on the bright side: less hair–less shampoo to buy, right?"

Elle rolled her eyes. "Whatever, but I'll never complain again about washing my hair–when I get to, I mean, which probably won't be for another thirty years."

That sucked. On a scale of one to ten, that was probably a negative ten.

"So they're going to send the right body?" Elle interrupted my thoughts. "What happens to the one in the freezer?"

My own sob caught, making words hard. "I, it's okay...he's gone, he'll never hurt you again. I'm sorry. Please don't cry."

She closed her one good eye, took a tiny breath, and glared at me. "Don't ever call me that, again. I never want to hear it–I never want to be reminded of him ever. Now please, what were we talking about?"

I cleared my throat. "So, you got to sit up in a wheelchair and you went for a ride?" I gulped as big a breath my sore ribs allowed. I will NEVER call her that, ever!

"Nope. They lifted me onto another bed that rolls, and I got wheeled to therapy, but at least it was outside this freakin' room."

"No way. How can you do physical therapy?"

"Not physical, dummy, mind-therapy." She tapped the good side of her head. "I guess it's psychotherapy. You know, when you've been through...what I've been through." She looked away.

"So, you going to do it more?" Suddenly my problems didn't seem so bad.

"I guess. Like, I have to talk about my dad and my mom and..." She darted a quick look at me. "Food and stuff." She stared out the window for a long time, after that. Finally, she turned back to look at me. "I don't want to A.J." Her mouth twisted into a sob.

I swallowed, hard. "Jeez, Elle, like, maybe it'll be good to, like, get it off your chest, you know?" I wished I could be anywhere on the planet but in that room. What was wrong with me? It was like I was saying, 'Sure, Elle, you were abused. Sure, you're anorexic. No big whoop. Talk about it to a stranger and you'll be healed'. Yeah, right.

Elle remained quiet for a long time, barely breathing as she folded the corner of the sheet–like a fan, unfolded, and refolded. "The shrink said it's probably all related."

I stared without moving a muscle; inside my head, the wheels rolled at the speed of sound. Mrs. Lawson, my sixth-grade science teacher, had said at 20 degrees Celsius, the speed of sound was approximately 343 meters per second or one mile in five seconds. Why did I think of that at a time like this? Why would I ever need to know that, anyway? I could barely run the vacuum cleaner.

"Hello? Where did you just go?"

I looked back at Elle. "Oh sorry; what does 'related' mean? Like, family-related?"

She shrugged. "Like one feeds off the other. Like I suffer from anorexia because of him...my, err, dad." She turned back to stare out that freakin' window, again. After a few minutes, she looked back at me. "Like I believe I'm fat because he forced me to suffer from low self-esteem, caused by, err, abuse." Her eyes flooded with tears. "Do you think that's possible? Do you believe I'm not fat?"

Finally, an opportunity to speak up–to get off my chest what I had longed to say ever since I first laid eyes on my new friend. "Elle, you are the most un-fat human being I know. As for the other stuff, who knows? It could be. Heck, I'm no shrink–I guess that's what shrinks get paid big bucks for...for knowing about weird brain stuff–how one thing causes something else. But one thing I do know, you're so not fat."

"Well, what do I have to lose?" Her eyes sparkled like ice crystals in sunshine, but her bottom lip quivered like Jell-O on steroids.

The only flip thing I could come up with—me, the Queen of one-liners—was, "So, you want to see whether or not studying for the Lit exam is related to an A?"

On a scale of one to ten, studying Literature any time is like waking up Christmas morning to a new game only to discover your parents forgot to buy batteries.

Chapter 11

Out Damned Spot! (And Other Useless Stuff Learned In School)

"Knock, knock." A blonde woman stuck her head into Elle's room.

"Aunt Gayle!" Elle lifted her one good arm toward the lady.

The blonde stranger looked a lot like Elle's mom, just an older version—same hair color, same eyes, but her eyes clouded with concern, her smile quivered. She rushed to Elle's bed and gently gathered her up in a tender hug, tears flowing down her cheeks.

"Hello, sweetheart." Aunt Gayle tossed me a look. "Hello. I'm sorry I'm such a mess, but I've been so worried."

"That's A.J.– remember I told you about her?" Elle was flat-out smiling, now.

She seemed so happy to see her aunt. If she was happy, I was happy. My toothy grin showed how happy.

"Of course, I do." Gayle smiled. "We finally meet, A.J. I hear you've got a crush on the star basketball player."

I suddenly lost my goofy grin. "Elle!" I looked at Aunt Gayle. "Like, not really. She's making it up."

"Not." Elle's eyes twinkled as brightly as her aunt's. "I'm not making it up. She so does."

"Oh, you are so full of it." I flung back, happy to have my old friend return, even if for a little while.

Gayle laughed. "I remember those days. He's probably BMOC, right?"

Elle's eyebrows shot toward the ceiling. Mine soon joined hers.

"BMOC-Big Man On Campus." Gayle shook her head. "Kids don't use that term now, I'm guessing. Well, popular, then."

"Duh," Elle said. "Like that must come from the dark ages."

"Well, whatever you say, I guess he's hot." Gayle crossed to the bedside table and plopped a large tote down, which she quickly unzipped. "I brought you something." Gayle pulled a squirmy object from the bag.

"No way!" Elle squealed. "A puppy! He's so cute! Gimme!" Her good arm reached out and her fingers wriggled in rhythm with the tiny parcel covered in a blanket.

My head jerked from Elle to the puppy and back again. My mind couldn't keep up with the action. I had no idea Elle could talk in exclamations. No way, her aunt smuggled a puppy into the hospital. I looked from one to the other. I had never seen Elle so excited.

"Shhhh!" Gayle shushed her niece. "You'll get us thrown out of here. Isn't it adorable?" She placed the wiggling, golden body gently on Elle's stomach and held it in place.

"What is he?" Elle's eyes never left the puppy.

"He's a *her*." Gayle smiled. "She's a Miniature Yorkie. I thought you'd want to name her, so I've been calling her 'Baby' because she's such a cute 'wittle baby. Aren't you? Aren't you a cute 'wittle baby-girl?" Gayle stood up. "I don't know how it's possible a tiny little nothing of a dog can make a grown person resort to baby talk, but she's sure won me over."

Elle's face lit up even more. "I get to name her? So, she's truly mine?" Her saucer-round eyes reminded me of those bouncing plates I'd once seen a juggler spin on sticks at the circus.

Gayle nodded. "She's yours. I bought her two days ago, and we've become great friends, but I told her all about her new owner–even showed her your picture. Unfortunately, she chewed the corner off, but she's smarter than the average dog. It's almost as if she understands exactly what I say." She leaned down to the small bundle still wrapped in the blanket. "Yes, you are, you're a smart puppy, aren't you? You're Aunt Gayle's amazing girl. And one day very soon, you're going to learn how to go potty on the pad, yes you are."

"I've never had a puppy before." Elle gently rubbed two fingers over the puppy's tiny back. "I think I'll call you

Lady Macbeth—then when I no longer have to yell 'out damned spot,' it'll mean you're all potty-trained."

I giggled and high-fived Elle's good hand. "Good one." I stroked the tiny dog's chin. "Lady Macbeth, you are so sweet, and I'd much rather hang with you than read about that other Lady M, any time."

Lady Macbeth did what any well-bred dog would do when it's the center of attention—she squatted on the pristine white sheet and, well, let's just say Elle will be yelling, "Out Damned Spot" for today, at least.

Elle tried her best to maneuver her broken body out of the way, but part of the sheet was covering her leg—the only part not covered by a cast. "Yuk! She tinkled on me! Get it off!"

Gayle grasped the tiny dog and suspended its wriggling body over a garbage can to complete its task. "Oh, Elle, honey I'm sorry! We'll clean you up, hold on."

At that very second, Nurse Busybody pushed back into the room. "Are we okay in here?"

I felt my liver and large intestine swap places, and I couldn't have uttered a coherent sentence if my life depended on it.

Gayle lowered Lady Macbeth into the garbage can. "Sure, we are, honey." She gestured to Elle. "But maybe you can bring us a clean sheet? We were giving her some water and, silly me, I spilled some on her leg."

The Nurse never took her eyes from her patient. "Sure. Give me that sheet, and I'll toss it in the laundry."

She yanked the sheet from the bed in one pull and rushed from the room.

My eyes trailed over Elle's battered body–probably the first time I'd seen her so exposed. Her one leg, poking out from under the hospital gown, sported a full-cast, but the other one was mostly blue and purple skin–the color of old bruises replaced by new ones. Somewhere deep inside, I heard a little voice saying she would hate for me to see her like this, but I couldn't make myself look away. I finally jerked back to reality when Elle burst out crying.

"But I don't want to move back to New York with you!"

Chapter 11

Typical

"What are you doing down here?"

The concern in Mom's voice broke my concentration from the fashion magazine. "Elle's Aunt Gayle is up in her room." I flipped my growing-out bangs behind one ear–which held a whole two seconds. "Figured I'd give them some time alone." I had hobbled out of Elle's room when she started sobbing about moving back to New York. Moving didn't seem like the end of the world to me; but then, I'd give my left kidney to live in New York.

Mom eased down in the chair beside me. "How did you carry your books on crutches?"

I glanced at my backpack. "Some guy helped me." I tried to act nonchalant, but my face burned hot. He definitely was not just 'some guy'–he was a total hottie.

"What guy?" The concern in Mom's voice upped three notches.

"Just somebody I met in the hall, no big deal." I pretended to read the magazine for real, now.

"How nice. Did you thank him?" Mom leaned toward me and kissed my cheek.

I jerked away, tossing a quick glance around the room. "Duh, of course, I thanked him. What do you think I am? A total moron?"

Mom pointed to my foot. "Your toes are turning blue." She leaned closer. "You need to prop your leg up more." She turned toward the elevator. "You ready to go home or did you plan to wait to see what's going on with Elle?"

Red Alert! I jerked my head up to peer at Mom. "Why? You know something."

Mom wouldn't meet my stare. "Oh, not much..."

"Mom!" I snatched her hand. "What's going on with Elle? Did her mother...?"

She heaved a deep sigh. "No, it's not about her mother–not totally, anyway. The latest report was she's still in a coma, and no one knows how long that will last, but they're hoping she wakes up soon. I guess every day is a day too long at this point."

I glanced back to the elevator, which by now, had become like some sort of bizarre link to Elle. "But what's going on with Elle? You know why her aunt is here? I mean, is she for real taking Elle back to New York? When will she go?" I stared at the metal doors like I half expected to see her come walking out. "Can Elle's aunt make her go back to New York and leave her mom here?"

"Calm down, honey." Mom began to gather up my books. "I guess that's between Elle and her aunt." She stood and reached out a hand to help me up. "Come on. They might take some time to sort things out."

"Mom, you know something. Tell me, please." I refused to budge from my chair.

Mom shrugged as if she carried a heavy load. She sat back down beside me. "Elle's aunt wants to take both Elle and her mom back to New York. To live."

A brick landed on my chest. "No!" My stomach flip-flopped. My eyes burned. *Life without Elle?* Not until that very moment had I known how much I needed her. "She can't go back." Tears pumped out of my eyes and poured down my face like a faucet. This was the worst day of my life—well, the worst one since being in Elle's basement.

I let Mom convince me to leave the hospital, leave Elle to deal with the heartbreaking news alone that she'd probably wind up moving back to New York. I failed to understand how that would be so bad. Surely things would be different now that her dad was dead.

I allowed Mom to help me up and I followed her to the car. Once inside, I leaned my head against the window and closed my eyes.

"Amanda Jo, are you listening to me?"

I looked out. We were headed downtown away from our house, toward...*toward the mall!*

I sat straight up in my seat. "Where are we going?"

"We're going to the mall to retrieve your backpack. There was a message on the machine this morning, not a very clear message, but sounded like someone found a backpack and traced it to you." Mom took her eyes off traffic for a second to glance my way. "Could it be yours? *Did* you lose your new backpack?"

My breath stuck in my throat. Mom didn't *sound* mad, no yelling, and no threats. She kind of seemed cool and calm. How could I get out of this? My heart pounded in my chest. I said the first thing that came to mind. "Uh, I loaned it to a friend to carry her books home, and uh, she didn't return it, yet."

The tiny lines between Mom's eyebrows sprouted wings. Apparently, that answer didn't make her very happy.

Wonder how she'd like the truth?

"You loaned your new backpack? The one I ordered online?" Mom's eyes glow in the dark when she's mad–even glow in bright sunlight, sometimes.

I mustered my most innocent voice, speaking in a dream-like whisper, like I did something good for somebody else, like Mother Theresa. "I didn't have books that day and truly thought she'd bring it back the next morning. Wasn't *my* fault she kept it." I crossed my fingers.

Mom didn't buy the innocent act. "I bought the backpack for you. Not for you to loan and then never get back." She expelled a deep breath. The kind that told me I was in trouble. "So, if this backpack is yours, you're telling me whoever you loaned it to just left it lying around somewhere at the mall?" She paused and then continued, "Serve you right if you never see it again. All that money down the drain. And when the old one wears out, you can see how much you enjoy carrying your books without one."

Her words punctured me like a nail in a tire, and I deflated as flat. I had let her down.

Which was worse—being accused of shoplifting or lying to your mom? I would soon find out.

Chapter 13

Lo Siento, Big Time

"Mr. Brown will see you now."

I skimmed sweaty palms down the legs of my jeans and blew out the breath I'd held. Who knew there was a boss over the whole mall?

"Amanda Jo?" Mom rose and marched toward the lady before she realized I hadn't. "You coming?"

I shook my head. "No. Why don't you go in without me?"

"Don't be silly. Get over here." Her index finger did a sharp half-circle. The tone in her voice filled in the blank: *now!*

My foot had taken on the weight of an anchor as I dragged it toward the door. I peeked inside the small office. There, in a brown leather chair, sat my new backpack. No denying it, now.

"Come in, come in." A little man motioned us inside. Little, because even though he stood, he was of the same height as most people sitting. "You must be Amanda Jo."

How did he know my name?

The man shook a finger in my face. "We've had a hard time tracking you down, young lady."

My heart did a perfect Salchow. He had tracked me down. Why had he needed to track me down?

Then, the heavy brick between my shoulders fell away and my fear flew out the window. Why? Was it because Mr. Brown was only as tall as I was? No, it had something to do with the smile on his face.

I shot him my biggest smile. "Well, here I am. Track no more."

Mr. Brown's smile broke into a laugh, and his whole body shook up and down in silent amusement, reminding me of that cartoon dog on TV. The next thing I knew, Mr. Brown had crossed over to where I was standing.

"Now, let me shake your hand and tell you how sorry I am about the misunderstanding."

What did he say? Was I dreaming?

Mom leaned in. "What misunderstanding? What's going on?" Her face sure wasn't filled with laughter.

Yeah, what misunderstanding? I wanted to ask the same question but thought better.

Mr. Brown walked back around his desk. "Is this your backpack?"

"Uh...could be."

Mom reached out a hand. "Amanda Jo, that's exactly like yours." She turned the flap over. "Yes, I'm sure it's your backpack. Did you have your name on yours?"

She stared at the tag. "There's no name, but it's your backpack, right?"

How would I get out of this? Maybe I could fake amnesia.

Mom appeared not to notice me freaking out. Turning to Mr. Brown, she asked, "Where did you find it?"

Mr. Brown motioned for us to sit. "Well, that's where it gets a bit sticky." He leaned forward in his chair. "It seems when we discovered the backpack, there was an item inside–a girl's sweater, to be exact." Mr. Brown paused and bored his eyes into mine. "You can understand how Ms. Lively made the mistake of thinking you intended to leave without paying, can't you?"

Mom jumped to her feet. "Now, you wait one minute."

"Mom...," I pulled her back down.

Mom leaned over Mr. Brown's desk, hands resting on the shiny surface, fingers pointing in every direction. "Now, you listen to me..."

I grabbed her shirt. "Mom, it's not what it seems."

Mom was on a mission. Was that fire shooting out of her ears? She straightened her shoulders, pulled up to her full height, and planted her hands on her hips. Mom was ready for battle. "My daughter is not a thief, and I demand an apology this instant."

Mr. Brown rose to his full 5'-ish height and held both hands out in front of his chest. "What I was trying to say is Ms. Lively misunderstood the entire situation." He turned to me. "The backpack does belong to you, correct?"

I nodded. Signed, sealed, and delivered.

"And you DID have the bag in your possession when Ms. Lively found you?"

Again, I nodded. Beam me up, Scotty.

Mr. Brown turned to Mom. "You can see how easy it was to assume your daughter put the sweater inside the bag, right?"

Mom, still in battle mode, charged ahead. "I can assume somebody accused an innocent young lady of shoplifting, I can assume if you'd asked the right person, you'd learn there's a reasonable explanation why that sweater was in her backpack, and I further can assume you should be asking the girl who borrowed the backpack in the first place."

"Mom..."

"Now, we're done here." Mom snatched the backpack out of Mr. Brown's hands and pulled me toward the door.

"Mom, wait!" Suddenly I found my voice and it bounced around the tiny office.

The look on Mom's face could have melted the iceberg that sunk the Titanic. "I'm waiting."

I opened my mouth, but this time the words stuck.

Mr. Brown broke the silence. "Why don't I give you some time to talk?" He started for the door. "Then, when you're all done, I'll come back and fill in some gaps."

Mom sat down and crossed her arms over her chest. Her right toe tapped repeatedly. "I said I'm waiting."

I swallowed. Once. Twice. "Mom, I know it seems bad..."

Tap. Tap. Tap. "Start from the beginning and don't leave anything out." Mom rigid body told me she meant it.

Leave anything out? Heck, I'd 'fess up about trying that cigarette in sixth grade if I thought it would help me right now.

Fifteen minutes later, and not one word from Mom, I'd told my side of the story–from not wanting to confront Lexi Lanthrope in the first place, to running for dear life when I got the opportunity. No time to skirt the truth now. I was in big trouble with Mom, and it was time to 'man up' and face the music–or the firing squad.

Mr. Brown chose that moment to rejoin us. "And have we finished with our little talk?"

Suddenly he didn't seem so small; instead, Mr. Brown seemed pretty big to me–about as big as the knot in my chest.

Chapter 14

Goodbye Friend

Mom jabbed a finger in the air. "One thing I don't understand is how did you know this backpack belongs to my daughter?"

Mr. Brown cleared his throat. "The real shoplifter confessed."

My head jerked up. "What?"

"Miss Lanthrope came forward." Mr. Brown smiled. "She arrived at my office last Friday with her parents, both of them."

Wait a minute, Lexi confessed?

Mom's eyes twitched. "Dr. Lanthrope, the doctor? And Dr. Lanthrope, his wife, the doctor?" Her mouth dropped open.

"The two and the same." Mr. Brown nodded.

He understood psychobabble. Turning his gaze on me, he continued, "Miss Lexi Lanthrope admitted she put the sweater in your backpack and alerted Ms. Lively. She also admitted *and paid for* several other items she'd taken out of the store that day and on other occasions." He paused and made a temple with his fingers. "Seems she'll be doing a lot of yard work over the summer."

I could just see that now–Lexi Lanthrope of the Walden Ridge Lanthropes, mowing yards while their gardeners played tennis.

Mr. Brown smiled again. "So, young lady, on behalf of Ms. Lively and the store, as well as the entire co-op, we owe you an apology. Please visit us here often." He stood and reached for my hand.

"Th...thanks." I shook his hand.

"What happened to your foot?" Mr. Brown asked.

Mom took Mr. Brown's hand next. "Long story, but she won't be running out the back door any time soon, nor will she be doing any shopping, here or anywhere else." She turned to me. "Young lady, you're so grounded."

What? Hadn't I just told the truth? A little late, maybe; but it wasn't like I had stolen anything. Besides, it was only a little white lie. "Mom…" I scrambled to stand, hopping on one foot.

"Don't 'Mom' me." She bent over and snatched up the hateful backpack–the one I'll never use again. She jabbed a finger at me. "You, in the car."

I don't ever remember seeing Mom that mad before. On a scale of one to ten, any chance of having a happy life vaporized right before my eyes–all because of one little white lie.

The car ride home was awful–worse than a lecture, worse than screaming and yelling, Mom didn't say a word, not one single, solitary, blessed word.

If my life sucked before, now it sucked slime juice, because, for the next three days, other than school, I spent every second in my room–no cell phone, no internet, no fun. Mom barely allowed me to visit Elle–and even then, she stood guard outside the door. Like, what am I, all of a sudden, a flight-risk?

"Your mom still mad at you?" Elle whispered on Tuesday.

Mom had picked me up after school and pointed the car downtown. I didn't dare ask where we were going, but last time that had happened we went to retrieve my backpack. I felt the relief roll down my spine when Mom turned the car into the hospital parking lot.

"She hates me–'might as well be dead,'" I whispered back, stealing a peek at the door.

Mom might not be in the room, but she lurked right outside, listening in on our conversation as if grounding me wasn't enough, she wanted to control me, too. Next, she would probably want to know my thoughts.

"So, you're still coming, right? To the airport" Elle interrupted my pity party.

"Yeah, I guess so. Still don't see why you have to leave, though."

"Not like I have a choice." Elle's mouth twitched.

"Maybe it won't be so bad–you get away from this place, at least." I swiveled another glance at the door.

"You're the one who wants to do that, not me."

"I know." I shrugged my shoulders. "Guess I'll see you on Thursday. Wish I could call you later, but I'll probably never get my phone back."

"It's okay." Elle quickly looked up at me and then back down to her phone. I couldn't help but wonder if she already had a new best friend to text. "See you Thursday." Her eyes never looked up again.

I left the room before she saw me cry.

On Thursday, Mom and Dad, who I still only answered in grunts, drove me to the airport to say goodbye to my best friend.

Chapter 15

Hello Cutie

Dad pulled his SUV up adjacent to the Rescue Van, and I stumbled out of the car as Elle's wheelchair rolled down the ramp. Before I reached her side, two paramedics had wheeled Mrs. Chambers' stretcher down the same ramp.

"You okay?"

"Couldn't be better." Elle's wrinkled nose and down-turned mouth screamed just the opposite.

"So, you got to ride with your mom, huh?"

"If you can call it that." She twisted her lips to one side. "Like she even knew I was there." A navy knit hat hid her scars and almost made her look normal–*almost*.

"She will soon." I was not good at small talk. I guess that's why they call it small. It generally means nothing.

A third paramedic walked up behind Elle and grasped the handles on her wheelchair. "Ready?"

"Couldn't be readier," Elle said in that same flip tone.

I fell into step behind Elle as the other paramedic rolled the still body of Mrs. Chambers toward the plane. I tried to keep my eyes glued straight ahead, but I couldn't help but glance at the rigid body lying on the gurney. Once, Mrs. Chambers was, hands-down, the most beautiful woman in the world, in the universe. Today, she looked like a ghost, and not the kind floating under a sheet on Halloween—the kind you see but wished you didn't.

Elle and I waited, without saying a word, while the two men loaded her mom on the plane. I deducted it would be just Elle, Mrs. Chambers, and a nurse on the flight to New York. I wiped away my tears and hugged my friend one last time. "Every day," I said in answer to her unspoken question.

She hooked her bent pinky with mine and repeated, "Every day."

The EMTs rolled Elle's chair backward up the ramp, and her eyes locked on me until the pilot slammed the door shut.

I starred at the plane until it became a silver pinpoint in the sky, and just like that, the best friend I'd ever known flew out of my life just as quickly as she had flown in.

"Let's go, honey." Dad put his arm around me and pulled me close. "Time for your therapy session. By the time you get finished, Elle'll be at her new home and you can write her on your phone, or whatever you call it."

"Text, Dad."

"Oh, right."

"Elle is where she belongs," Mom said. "And you're where you belong." Her stern look told me I was still in big trouble, and now wasn't the time to whine.

I had become a pro at hobbling myself into the backseat of the car and stowing my crutches in beside me, but today wasn't one of those days. A river of sweat rolled down my back as I'd twisted and swung my butt inside. Then to add insult to injury, I dropped a crutch outside the car. With one foot in, one foot out, there was no way I could retrieve it on my own. That feeling of helplessness sucked a whopping forty million.

"Here, let me help." The voice sounded slightly familiar.

I looked up to see the hot guy from the hospital–the day Elle's aunt dropped by to tell her they were moving to New York, the day I hopped out of Elle's room, trying to balance books and the knowledge that my best friend in the entire world might be dropping out of my life for good. The one who had helped me with my books.

He turned his head to the left. "Say, I know you." He turned my crutch around, tip first, and eased it into the car beside me. "How's the homework coming?"

"It's coming. Thanks for helping." I could feel Mom and Dad staring at me. "Mom, Dad, this is....what was your name, anyway?"

"Clay. Clay Watson."

"A.J." I flashed him my best smile.

Mom 'harrumphed' from the front seat.

"Thanks, young man." Dad turned around to look at Clay.

"Yeah, thanks, but what are you doing here?" I looked at the spot where the plane had sat, then back at Clay. "You work here?"

"No. Not here. I work after school with EMT–as an intern. I plan to go into pre-med after graduation, so I'm racking up community points. I'm hoping to work during the summer at the hospital. That's what I was doing there when your books had a collision with the floor."

"Oh, cool." At first, I couldn't think of another word to say; then my curiosity got the best of me. "So why are you here–now I mean?"

"We transported a patient to the airport. I got to observe."

"Mrs. Chambers–she's my friend's mom, and my friend, Elle in the, err, wheelchair–it was Elle's room I'd just left when I dropped my books." Small world.

"Amanda Jo, we really need to go to your P.T." Dad looked in the rearview mirror.

Clay backed away from the car. "Oh, sorry." He looked me in the eyes. "Like, maybe I'll see you around this summer."

"Yeah, like maybe."

"Look, I'm on FacePage," Clay said. "Page me."

Dad put the car into gear and rolled forward.

My head hung out the window, like a long-haired Cocker Spaniel, my hair whipping around my face. "I will. So am I. Page me in case I forget." As if…

Of course, Mom couldn't let it go. "You don't even know him, Amanda Jo, and you are too young to be friends with boys."

"How could I be too young to have friends?"

"You know nothing about him. He could be a serial killer, for all you know. What's FacePage, anyway?" Mom turned around to look me in the face. "And what are you doing on it?"

According to Mom, the world is made up of serial killers–half of them live in our neighborhood, and the other half live on the Internet. They're not real people, just lurkers in cyberspace.

I knew weirdos lurked on the Internet, but I was always careful. I knew better than to put personal info out there. I knew better than to chat up strangers. However, the most important thing I knew was not to let Mom read my personal page.

"Answer the question. What's face paging? You don't have a pager unless it's on your cell phone."

Mom had no clue. I rolled my eyes. I was stuck in mid-warp. My parents live in the past. I continually drag them, kicking and screaming, to the present. Forget about the future.

"Maybe it's like the writing they do on their cell phones, kind of like email on the computer, but not exactly."

Dad had no idea what he was talking about. Hadn't I just told him I would text Elle later? I tuned both of them out while they discussed 'Technology 101 meets Morse code'. I could see it was going to be a long car ride. My life had gone from sad to pitiful in a matter of days, and there was no end in sight. It would be four more weeks before the cast came off. Four more weeks of crutches, taking a sponge bath, and zero fun.

When we finally arrived at the hospital, Dad helped me out of the car. "I'm going to park, but we'll be in the waiting room when you get finished. Are you sure you don't need help getting upstairs?"

"I'm fine." I didn't even look back. I focused on the gray concrete building in front of me, the gray concrete asphalt under me, and the gray concrete-like sky, above. Even the blue sky had abandoned me. I hobbled over to the elevator and used the tip of my crutch to poke the 'up' button.

"Hey, you."

Chapter 16

Diva Moves and Other Things I Learned From My Fav Celebrities

Clay Watson!

"Hey." I stopped breathing for several seconds, and then gulped air like a fish on the riverbank. "What are you doing here?"

Mom's voice echoed through my mind: 'Don't slump, Amanda Jo!' I pulled myself up to my full height. For once, Mom was right. I *do* slump.

Clay held the elevator door open for me. "Are you sure you don't need any help?" His voice spilled with true concern, not the accusing kind from my parents when I say I'm too sick to clean my room.

"Oh, trust me, I'm an old pro at this. So, what are you doing here? Didn't I just leave you at the airport?"

He laughed and followed me into the elevator. "Remember, I told you I'm applying for summer work here?" He paused to look at me. "You're going to third, right?"

I nodded my head. He remembered! That MUST mean something. Maybe he came here just to see me? Wait 'til I tell Elle! Oh, Elle's not here anymore.

Clay pushed the button for the third floor and then six. "Well, I really like the ER. I'm here to see if I could qualify for a new summer program the school is sponsoring. If so, I thought I'd try to get a jump on it. It would sure look good on college applications."

So much for coming to see me. "Yeah right, Sherlock. Get it? Watson–Sherlock?" How lame! What was I–twelve?

The elevator door chose that minute to open. I would probably get stuck in an elevator at least once in my life, but not today. No, today, the elevator had to work perfectly.

Clay laughed. "That's good. But about the program–I doubt I can get in, but somebody will. Why not me?" He held the door for me to shuffle out.

My face burned hot. "I didn't mean...I mean...like..."

"It's all good. I know what you meant. It was funny–Sherlock Holmes and Dr. Watson. I get it. If everything falls into place, I could be Dr. Watson one day. Or I could get into the program and realize it's not for me. Won't know until I try."

I hobbled out of the elevator. "Well, good luck. I'm late for P.T. Catch you later." I tossed my hair like I'd seen Miley Cyrus do in one of her videos.

"Yeah. Maybe I'll hang and we can grab a Coke afterward."

I remembered my folks waiting downstairs. "Uh, don't think I can today–maybe this weekend?" Oh boy! Did I just invite a boy on a date? Mom would throw a fit.

"Sure." He appeared not to notice my embarrassment. "I have to work ten hours Saturday, but I'm off Sunday."

So far, so good. I tossed my hair again, and once more, simply because it felt good. "Great. I'll page you. Maybe later today." My cool factor was at an all-time high.

"Make it after nine. I'll be home by then."

"Later." I swung down the hall but turned to flash him my sexiest-pouty-Madonna smile and another head toss. It seemed like hours before the elevator door closed, taking away my view of the cutest boy, ever–even cuter than Bryant Baker. And this one likes me, not Lexi Lanthrope.

When I arrived at P.T., I couldn't help but sneak a look in the mirror hanging on the opposite wall.

My heart did a nosedive. My hair stuck straight up on top–like a giant woodpecker. I bet every time I tossed my head, it flapped like the school's gigantic American flag on a windy day. I glanced at myself in the mirror again and raked my fingers through my stupid hair. Note to self: leave the princess act to Lexi and her goons. I rushed through therapy and hobbled back into the elevator.

When the doors opened, Mom smiled like she was happy to see me. She even handed me my cell phone.

"What? I get to text Elle and give it right back?"

Mom held her hand up. "It's yours, again. For now. Keep the battery charged and don't give me a reason to take it back. Understand?"

I nodded, cupping my hand around the phone before she reneged. I twisted around to make sure Clay was nowhere in sight. I couldn't face him right now. He would surely think I was the biggest dork that ever lived. I swung into the lobby and out to the car, behind Mom and Dad.

I felt different, though. Even Mom didn't get on my nerves on the ride home. For some reason, I experienced tinglings of a calmer, quieter me—borderline maturity, even. Maybe it's because I *might* have a boyfriend. I might *soon* be in a relationship.

Finally, back in my room, I curled up in bed, grabbed my phone, and clued Elle in on my date for Sunday.

Right on cue, she responded. *UR Mom will spaz
#Not telling her
*UR meeting him @ Mall Sunday?
#Y if I can
*Mom will drop u off?
#Telling her meeting g'friend
*B careful
#K. Ttyl

Texting Elle was not like having her here, but it was better than nothing, and I knew I could count on her to help me figure out a plan to get Mom to take me to the mall

Sunday–that's what friends do; oh, yeah, that and not let friends drive drunk.

Chapter 17

Apology Accepted

Mom stuck her head in my room. "Somebody to see you downstairs."

"Who is it?"

"Lexi Lanthrope."

My heart froze. "What does she want?"

"You need to ask *her* that. Plus, you need to thank her for clearing your name at the mall." Her eyes curdled three shades darker.

"She started it. She owes *me* an apology for shoplifting that sweater and trying to pin it on me–if she hadn't stuck that sweater in my backpack, I wouldn't have any reason to thank her."

"Amanda Jo, go see what she has to say, and be nice." There was that look, again.

Sure enough, Lexi Lanthrope was waiting for me in the big hallway downstairs, sure enough, she looked like she was sorry for what she did, and sure enough, I got a big lump in my throat.

"Hey, how's the ankle?"

"Getting there." I hobbled over to the bench under the stairway. "Want to sit?"

Lexi followed. "Sure, but I can't stay long." She sat on the edge of the bench as if she wanted to bolt at any second. "I've got 'beaucoup' chores around the house." She straightened a stray wisp of hair and dusted her shoulder. "So, how's Elle? You heard from her?"

"Yep. She's okay. Missing here, but I guess she didn't have a choice."

"What about her mom?"

"You know about what happened?" I darted a quick sideways look.

"Yeah, everyone's been talking about it. Like, it was all over the news."

"Bad deal."

"Who knew?" Lexi extended her hands, palms up. "Her dad must have been a monster."

"Yeah, like, Elle tried to hide it, even from me, but I saw stuff. I knew something wasn't right, you know?" I glanced toward the front door, knowing full-well Jay was dead and wouldn't walk through any door again, but old habits are hard to break. I tossed another look back at Lexi. "And Elle, she acted like two different people sometimes. I probably shouldn't be talking about it."

"I know. I feel the same way, and I told the gang we shouldn't be talking about it like it was funny—it's not. Nobody should have to live like that. I feel sorry for her."

"Don't!" My hand jerked out as if I'd held it too close to a bonfire. "Don't feel sorry for Elle. She would hate that."

Lexi nodded. "You're probably right, but I don't know how else to feel. It just makes me sad."

"Sad is okay, sorry for her not so much."

"Well, sorry is probably how I should feel about what I did to you at the mall. Like, how stupid was I?"

Uh oh, here it came. The epic apology.

"I mean, like, I feel like a moron for cramming that sweater in your backpack." She splayed her hands. "Not right then, but later, when I realized that, you know what? It's not cool, after all. It's dumb." She paused as if remembering exactly when she realized her mistake. "Oh sure, I felt cool in front of Jen and Blair, but later, when I was alone, I felt bad, I promise."

Was she going to cry? I concentrated on a speck on my sleeve. "Well, it *was* a pretty mean thing to do." Why didn't I feel good? She was feeling bad, and I should be happy. What was wrong with me?

"I know. Trust me, I know." Lexi rubbed at her eyes and sniffed.

Two signs of tears—the old 'rubbing and sniffing trick'. I made the big Lexi Lanthrope cry! Why didn't I feel good?

Lexi looked around. "This place is creepy. Oh, I'm sorry, but does it ever give you the creeps?" Her cheeks turned the same color as her nose.

"It's okay." Did I just say that living over a funeral home was okay? What was happening with me today?

"I mean, it's pretty, just a little creepy. Cool, too, sort of."

"Yeah, Home Sweet Home." I stuck my cast out in front of me.

"So, listen, I'm sorry for what I did at the mall. I told Mom and Dad, and they took me down there, and I told this guy. He's like the manager or something; anyway, he said he'd explain everything to your parents and return your bag. They know you are innocent in the whole thing." She wiped her eyes, again.

"I know. Mom took me down there, already. Mr. Brown said you came in. Did you really shoplift all that other stuff?"

Lexi's eyes flashed in my direction and then straight ahead. "Yeah. Dumb, huh?"

By now, I'd lost all sense of trying to be unruffled. "Why did you do it? Like, you have money to buy stuff."

Lexi rolled her eyes. "Fun, I guess, only we both know how much joy it truly brought." She bent over and re-tied her already perfectly-tied laces on her tennis shoes. She swallowed several times. "Like I said, I thought it made me look smart or something, but it only made me look stupid."

I blinked several times. My eyes stung as if I'd stared too long at the sun.

"Even Jen and Blair tried to get me to put the stuff back, but it's like I couldn't stop." She grew quiet for a moment. "I really wanted that stuff bad, until I took it. Then I didn't want it anymore." She turned to me. "Sick, huh?"

I couldn't let it go. "But, again, you had the money to pay for it, didn't you? I mean, if you'd wanted to buy it, you probably could have."

Lexi shrugged her shoulders, crossed her arms over her chest, and cleared her voice before speaking, "That wasn't the point. It was as if I craved the excitement of taking stuff *without* paying. I know it was foolish, now; then it seemed exhilarating." Her eyes teemed up, emptied, and then filled up again. "You wouldn't understand. I'm not sure I do. Maybe I have bad blood from, uh, from…you know who."

I pointed to the table on the other side of the room. "There's a box of Kleenex on that table. I'd get it for you, but you'd be done crying by the time I got back."

"Thanks." Lexi scooted off the bench and walked to the table.

Even when her nose was a dead-ringer for Rudolph's, and her face was blotchy red, Lexi Lanthrope still managed to look good.

After a few delicate nose-blows, she returned to the bench. "Like, I know how stupid it was, and I'm sorry. I just want you to know I think you're a better person than me–than I was, I mean. I hope I've learned from how dumb I acted, and I hope I can be a better person someday. God knows I'm trying." She looked me in the eye. "Like, I don't want to turn up like my, err, real mom, if you can call her that." She rolled her eyes straight up and dropped her shoulders. "Please, don't let me turn out like her, please let me be somebody my Grandmother would have been proud of."

Up until then, I had been able to hold it all in. Now, those stupid tears were stinging my eyes. Stupid tears! Blink. Blink. Blink. Of course, that didn't work. No matter what, I was going to actually cry. I swallowed hard. "It's okay. I was pretty mad." I stopped a tear running down my face. "But I'm over it."

"Here." Lexi laughed, handing me the tissue box.

"Thanks," I snorted. "I don't know why I'm crying. Stupid too, I guess."

"There's a lot of that going around." Lexi smiled.

We sat there like two dumb bunnies, sniffing, laughing, and wiping tears with that dumb box of Kleenex.

"Hey, I'm going to the mall Sunday." Lexi wiped a final tear from the corner of her eye. "Want to come?"

Cha-Ching. "Sure." Things were looking up.

How wrong could I be?

Chapter 18

BF4L

Me: How's life?

Elle: Not so bad

Me: Gr8. Like UR room?

Elle: It's ok. Yellow. Do I look like a yellow chick?

Me: U didn't look like a pink & purple 1, either

She and I were chatting on FacePage, while she filled me in on her life in New York–the place of my dreams, the Big Apple, paradise.

Elle: Ma-b u can visit N summer

Me: Ma-b. Doubt it, tho

Elle: Y?

Me: Mom thinks I'm a screw-up

Elle: U CN ask

Me: Tru. I can ask

Elle: So, u & Lexi. Who knew?

Me: No biggie. She apologized. I didn't say we'd b friends

Elle: Going to mall, tho

Me: Hey, I'm not hanging w/her. Going to c Clay. U know TH@

Elle: Just saying

Me: L8ter, g8ter

Elle: Let me know WH@ he says

Me: K

I'd looked up Clay's homepage earlier, I knew how to page him. All I needed to do was hit the keys. Why was I stalling?

Clay: Ping

What? It was him!

Me: Hey, dude

Clay: U ok?

Me: Yep

Clay: Bad time?

Me: N

Clay: k

Me: k

This wasn't going so well. Why couldn't I think of something to say?

Clay: We still on 4 Sunday?

Me: Yep

Clay: Cool. Want me to pick u up?

Panic!

Me: uh..already planned to B @ mall. U come there?

How old is he, anyway? You big dummy! Mom would die if she knew he already has his license and a car. Why didn't I think he'd have his license if he had a job?

Clay: cool. C U @ 5 or so

Me: works 4 me

Now what?

Sometimes texting or paging just won't work. I punched in Elle's number.

"A.J.?"

"Great. You're awake."

"What's wrong?" She sounded sleepy.

"I just agreed to meet Clay Sunday, at the mall."

Elle yawned in my ear. "Yeah? So? Wasn't that the plan?"

"So, it just dawned on me; like, he's older than me. He has a car."

"Didn't you think that maybe he had a car? Most people do, you know. Like, he has a job, for crying out loud."

"I guess I didn't get past how cute he is."

"So, what are you going to do?"

"About the mall? I guess I'm still going. It's not like I'm only going to just meet up with him. Besides, he's probably only two years older than me. That's not so bad."

"Your mom probably won't agree. But who'd thought you and Lexi Lanthrope would turn out to be friends?"

"It's no big deal. Like, she'd told the mall it wasn't me, remember? I told you all that."

I could hear Elle's sigh, loud and clear. "Yeah, so now she's come over and you're BFFs, right?"

"NOT! But I can't get over the fact Lexi apologized to me for acting like I stole the sweater. And for setting me up."

"Weird."

"Ya' think? You're still my BFF. And my BF4L."

"Me, too," Elle said, "if it's possible to be a best friend for life while living a thousand miles apart."

"That part sucks, but not forever, remember? I'm moving to New York one day and going to be a fashion designer."

"Not soon enough."

Being separated from your BF4L sucks on a scale of one to ten...a major ten. "True."

Elle yawned. "Remember everything that happens Sunday. I so wish I was there."

"I will tell you everything. I promise." A huge yawn built in my chest and escaped out my mouth. "Well, 'most everything."

"Already, you like him more than me."

"No way!"

"Seems like it."

I laughed. "You're always going to be my best friend, remember? That's what BF4L means–'best friend for life.'"

"Even over Lexi?"

"Especially over Lexi."

I fell asleep with a picture of Elle waving to me from the top of the Statue of Liberty, as I ran up a long, winding stairway screaming, "Best Friend For Life, Best Friend For Life!"

Chapter 19

Up The Creek Without A Crutch

Sunday finally arrived, and it was time to broach the subject of going to the mall. "So Mom, Lexi Lanthrope invited me to hang at the mall this afternoon. Can I go?"

Mom had withdrawn the grounding part when she finally realized I was the victim, but she still barely allowed me out of her sight.

"When did you and Lexi Lanthrope become such good friends?" The frown lines between her eyebrows grew by several inches.

"We're not. Just when she was here, remember? She asked me if I wanted to hang at the mall today. It's not like I have a lot of friends, especially since Elle left. Besides, I think Lexi is truly sorry, and I'm afraid she'll think I don't truly forgive her if I don't go."

Mom covered the pot she had been stirring and wiped her hands. "I know it's been rough on you since that day in Elle's basement. It has been rough on all of us." She poured herself a cup of coffee. "I force myself not to think about it. That poor, poor girl." She stared into space for a long minute, then shook her head. "What Elle and her mother must have endured, not to mention what he did to you…"

Sure enough, here came the waterworks.

"Mom, don't. If you cry, I cry. Besides, you always say: All's well that ends well."

"I know, I know." Mom dabbed the dishcloth at her eyes.

"So, the mall? Can I go?"

"I guess, but you better promise me no hanky-panky."

"Like, what am I going to do in this shape?" Mentally, I crossed my fingers behind my back.

"I'm not kidding. No funny stuff."

"No hanky-panky or funny stuff." I nodded my head.

After lunch, I loaded the dishes in the dishwasher, carried my laundry to my room (hopped it in is a better description), and straightened up the living room. When four o'clock arrived, I reminded Mom it was time to go.

When we pulled up to the front entrance, and after rehashing every safety rule known to mankind, she finally agreed to let me go in by myself to find Lexi.

"We're meeting at the front door," I lied. You'd think I'd learn a lesson by now. "No point in finding a parking place just to turn around and come back to the car; besides, it's a shorter walk if you drop me off." That part was true, at least.

"If you're worried about walking, you surely don't need to traipse all over the mall then." She had me there.

I took a deep breath. "Okay, I'm not worried about the walking. I just don't want my mommy coming in with me. I'm not a baby, you know."

Mom grinned. "Oh, afraid I'll embarrass you, huh?"

"Seriously, Mom—they'll think I'm a baby."

"All right, I hear you." She pulled up to the door and waited while I swung my foot out and balanced on my crutch.

I winced in pain when the padded end made contact with the tender skin of my underarm—like fire licking a wound, but I certainly wasn't going to let on. Nothing would stop me from seeing Clay Watson, not my tender armpit, not Lexi Lanthrope, not even Mom.

"What time do I need to be back?" Mom asked.

"I'll call."

"No, what are your plans and how long do you intend to stay?"

"Mom, can I just call you?"

She tapped her fingers on the steering wheel. She did that a lot—tap, tap, tap. "I need to know what time you plan to come home, and I'm not moving until I do." Tap, tap, tap.

"Fine. seven...eight?"

"I'll be here at six-thirty." Mom looked at me and pointed down with her index finger. "Right here."

"Fine." I step-swung toward the entrance.

Mom was so weird. I would never get to do anything as long as I lived in this crummy town. Just wait until I move to New York. I'll show her. I'll never come back–not even on her birthday, not even Christmas. Heck, not even on Thanksgiving…and especially not New Year's Eve. That's when they do the ball-drop thingy in Times Square. Can't miss that.

"Well, hello there, sweetheart. Need some help?"

I jerked my head up. "Hi. No, I'm used to it."

A guy dressed in black jeans, black tee, and silver necklaces rushed to open the door. "Let me get the door. After you, m'lady." He freakin' bowed.

Normally, it would have been geekish, but he was very cute–not cute like Clay but cute in a different way. "Thanks."

Goth Guy smiled. Perfect teeth. "You need help getting where you're going?"

"Nope. I'm meeting friends, and I can make it, but thanks, again." I swung inside, looking for the nearest seat. The dang crutch genuinely hurt my underarm, now.

"Why don't I walk with you until you find your friends?" The guy stepped in front of me, blocking my way.

"It's okay, really." I darted a quick look around. "I'm meeting my friends right here."

He swung around, then looked back. "I don't see anyone, maybe they're at the arcade."

"Maybe."

Beep. Beep. Beep.

I dug my cell phone out of my pocket. *Clay!*

*Sorry. Can't make it. Got called in 2 work. Ttyl

"Are you kidding me?" I crammed my phone back into my pocket. "Dang it!"

"Sounds like you got a problem. How about we sit down and talk–over here?" He gestured toward a nearby bench.

I hopped along behind him. Now, my good foot was aching, not to mention my armpit, and I really needed to sit.

The guy stopped. "Or we don't have to sit. I have a car. We can drive to the other side of the mall and get some food. There's a Mickey Dee's behind the mall."

"I don't even know your name."

"Slide. My homies call me Slide. What's yours?"

"A.J."

"A.J...what does it stand for?"

"It stands for A.J." I tried to sound equally hip. "My homies call me A.J."

Slide nodded. "That's what I'm talking about. So, you want to head?"

Something crawled up my back, like a spider. What was that nursery rhyme? 'Along came a spider and sat down beside her'.

"I really shouldn't." Part of me wanted to–not that he was anybody I'd ever be interested in. He was just here, and Clay wasn't. Neither was Lexi from what I could tell. And Elle...don't even get me started about Elle. What harm would it do? A person only goes around once, right? "You know what? Why not?"

Slide smiled. "That's what I'm talking about. I'll have you back whenever you say—nobody needs to know."

"Right. But I have to be back. You will have me back in an hour, right?"

"Sure."

Slide's car was a clunker, but it ran. We rolled the windows down, and he cranked up the music. I'd never cruised before, but it didn't take long before I understood the attraction. Soon, my head was rocking to the rhythm vibrating from the back seat speakers, and the more people that looked at us, the better I felt.

"That's what I'm talking about." Slide kept repeating those words over and over; and for some unknown reason, they were the funniest words I'd ever heard. Once, when Mom's face popped into my mind, I pushed it away and laughed harder—that was until I realized Slide had left the mall parking lot and was pulling onto the freeway.

"Where are you going?" I sat straight up as panic set in. I turned my head, side-to-side, like some kind of dummy.

"No sweat. We're going to another cruising spot—a better place than the mall. No cops, just a bunch of my homies."

I sat up straighter. The boom-ba-ba boom was now hurting my head, and I had trouble stringing two thoughts together. I said the next thing that popped into my head, "Mom will be looking for me. She's probably had time to park the car by now. I probably should go back."

Slide threw me a look. "You said she just dropped you off. We'll ride over there, see my friends, and breeze right back. No problem."

"You sure?" My mouth went dry, and I wanted out of this car in the worst way.

"Relax. We'll be back in a flash."

"I guess…"

"Relax." Slide leaned over and pulled a plastic bag from under the seat. "Here, fix me up."

I looked at the bag he'd tossed in my lap. "What is it?"

Slide smiled. "Just a little weed. No biggie."

"I…I don't smoke weed. And you shouldn't, either."

"Come on. Roll me up one."

How could I not see what a loser he was? How dumb could one girl be? Before I could respond, Slide pulled the car off the road and turned into a vacant lot.

My fear turned to panic. "What are you doing? Where are the others?"

"If you can't help me out, I'll do it myself. We'll park under this shade tree for a little while. Nice vacant parking lot, huh?" He shifted the car in park and cut off the motor.

I watched in shock as he rolled a joint and lit the tip. Immediately, a sickly-sweet smell filled the car. I gagged and swallowed bile.

"You've never had any of this before, have you? Girl, where've you been all your life? Here, watch me."

He put the end of the joint in his mouth and sucked. He then clamped his mouth together and held his breath for several seconds. When he opened his mouth, barely any smoke at all came out. "Boo-ray! Oh, baby, that's sweet." He stuck the nasty stuff in my face.

I pushed him away. "Leave me alone!"

"Aw, come on baby, just a little toke."

"Get that away from me, and take me back to the mall, now." On a scale of one to ten, my luck sucked zero–how would I get out of this?

"Come here, sweetheart." Slide held the joint with one hand and pulled me toward him with the other.

I pushed him away. "Get off me. Let go!"

"Don't be like that–I just want to kiss you." He grabbed the back of my hair and yanked me forward.

Wrong move. The last person who grabbed me by my hair almost killed me. Without thinking, I slammed my fist right into his nose, hard. Blood spurted out all over Slide's black shirt, on the steering wheel, and onto his jeans.

"You crazy or what? Look what you've done."

Horrified, I watched blood spurt between his fingers.

"Get out!"

I yanked the door handle so hard it came off in my hand. For some reason, I had sense enough to reach outside to open the car door. I stumbled out–literally, hit the pavement, and rolled away from the speeding car that left black marks all over the concrete–the speeding car with my crutch still inside.

I hopped over to the concrete wall that boxed in the shade tree and plopped down, exhaling a shaky breath. I was happy to be out of that car, happy to be away from that jerk, happy to be alive; but also stranded.

Beep. Beep. Beep. Thank God for cell phones! I dug mine out of my pocket. *Clay!*

*Hey. Can u call me?

Ring.

"Clay! Thank God! I need help!"

"Hey girl, slow down. What's wrong?" Clay's voice sounded like the best song that ever rocked the charts.

"I did something stupid, and now I'm stranded without a crutch; I can't hop all the way back to the mall." Tears stung my eyes. That's all I needed, to start bawling like a baby.

"I thought you were *at* the mall. Where are you?"

I looked around. "Over by the old baseball field—you know, the one by the theater?"

"I'll be there in ten."

"Hurry!"

Chapter 30

Lucky Stars
(The Ones Above...Not The Cereal)

"Do you even know how stupid that was?" Elle's voice shrieked from New York.

When I felt it was safe, I pulled the phone back to my ear. "I know it was stupid, and I also know you almost burst my eardrum."

"Somebody needs to burst your head; talk about luck. The real luck was when Clay texted you, and you still had your cell phone–that's twice we owe our lives to a phone."

I closed my eyes. "Like I could ever forget. I'll carry that nightmare around with me forever." When I realized how that sounded, I rushed on. "Hey, I'm sorry. You've been carrying more than that, but that's right, you saved both our lives with your cell phone; and today, my battery was actually charged when I needed mine. How lucky was that?"

"A.J., you can't always count on luck, you know. Sometimes, you've got to stop and think before you do stupid stuff. Like, you need to weigh the consequences. If it feels wrong, it probably is, right?" She blew out a breath, but I still held mine.

She's right—I need to grow up.

"So, when Clay picked you up...was he mad? I hope he chewed your butt out."

This time, I blew out my breath and bit back the sob that threatened to prove just how scared I truly was. "Well, h-he said that he g-got to work at the same time as the other guy, the one who was supposed to work. He just showed up late, I guess." I blinked away the hateful tears and pushed a pillow under my tired foot—not the one with the cast, the one that had hopped me over half of the town today. It was quiet in my room. The TV was still on, but Mom and Dad were asleep, and I felt safe, for now at least.

"So, then what happened?" Elle goaded me to tell her the full story.

I sighed. "When Clay picked me up, he drove me back to the mall, and I called Mom to come pick me up."

"Did she ask you why you didn't stay?"

"I told her I was tired of hopping around on one foot, and that maybe it was too big of a challenge, after all." I looked toward the door to make sure Mom wasn't eavesdropping. "You know how parents love it when you admit you're wrong."

Elle was quiet for a second. "I miss that."

Could I be any more stupid?

After a few seconds, she asked, "What about your missing crutch?"

"I told Mom I'd left it propped up against a wall when we got a coke, and when I went back to get it, it was gone."

"And she didn't go ballistic?"

"I didn't say that. I got the big lecture all the way home about how I'm not responsible, how I need to pay more attention, how I still have a lot of growing up to do."

"You do."

"I know. I do have a lot of growing up to do. Gosh Elle, how stupid was I to get in that car?"

"You could have seriously been hurt."

I snagged my quivering lip between my teeth. "Tell me about it. I'll probably have nightmares for the rest of my life." Tears stung my eyes, for real, this time.

"You're lucky, that's for sure. For crying out loud, A.J, am I going to have to come back there and watch out for you?"

"Wish you could." That funny feeling crept back into my throat—the one where you know you could cry any minute, or not.

"Well, I wasn't going to say anything…"

"What?"

"Nothing's positive."

I sat up. "What?"

"Quiet or you'll wake up your Mom, and you might have to explain what really happened at the mall."

"True, but what were you trying not to say?"

"Like I said, nothing is worked out, but Aunt Gayle says she might have made the wrong move in bringing Mom back to New York."

"But where would she go?"

"I asked that same question. Seems there's this place near Mill Oak that's somehow connected to the hospital there. And get this, Aunt Gayle says Mom's doctor here said that Dr. Lanthrope is on staff there and has been working with coma patients."

"Him or her?"

"Her. I told Aunt Gayle I know the Lanthropes. I guess I kind of made it sound like we were tight."

"So are you saying you might move back here?" I held my breath.

"No, I didn't say that. I don't have a clue if Aunt Gayle is even seriously considering it. I just said we talked about it. She did say that she couldn't think about sending Mom off somewhere by herself. That's when I suggested we come down there for a few days and check out the facility. Aunt Gayle said she'd have to think about it some more, but at least, she's considering bringing me back for a visit to look at the facility. That's better than nothing."

The sun popped out and the birds began to sing–in my bedroom, in the middle of the night. "Wow. Like, can you…are you able to travel?"

"In a wheelchair for now, but no longer bed-ridden. Aunt Gayle said we could drive. You know, stop a lot. Make it fun." She paused for a minute. "Remember, nothing is for sure, but I begged and begged for her to think about making a permanent move. She agreed to think about it."

I exhaled loudly. "That sounds almost *too* good."

"Like I said, it's not a done deal. I just made sure Aunt Gayle knows how happy it would make me, and she says my happiness will figure into her decision. We're a family now and she said she will think about what I want, too."

"Woohoo! That would be the best thing in the world. I can't believe she'd even consider it–living in New York all her life, and all."

After a long pause, Elle spoke quietly. "Well, Aunt Gayle says a house with a backyard is beginning to sound better than a three-story walk-up, especially since it's a long subway ride every day to see Mom. I keep telling you, New York isn't the most fabulous place to live. It's cool, but it's not the end of the world."

"I guess." I still wasn't convinced. "Like, I've been thinking lately that fashion designing has lost some of its magic, too. Matter of fact, I've decided to tell Mom what happened today, come clean, you know?"

"Wow. Let me know how THAT works out."

"I need to grow up. I thought maybe that might be a good way to begin the process."

"I guess..." Elle's voice trailed off.

I rushed on. "Like, I'm going to see what she thinks about me, maybe, volunteering at the hospital this summer. Who knows? Medicine might be something I'm interested in." That and Clay Watson. It wasn't like I dreamed about College all my life, but if I applied to one nearby, Mom surely would be happy.

"A.J., you still there?" Elle's voice sliced through my daydream.

"I'm still here, g' friend." I stifled a huge yawn. "And I'm not going *anywhere*." I snuggled down on my pillow and a huge smile crept over my face. For the first time in a long time, I loved my life. On a scale of one to ten, it was a freakin' 10!

Author's Note:

If you or someone you love is living with abuse, help is only a phone call away. For local assistance, dial 911. Many agencies are standing by, ready to help. Below are only two:

ARCH National Respite Network and Resource Center
4016 Oxford Street
Annandale, Virginia 22003
Phone: (703) 256-9578
http://www.archrespite.org
The mission of the ARCH National Respite Network and Resource Center is to assist and promote the development of quality respite and crisis care programs; to help families locate respite and crisis care services in their communities; and to serve as a strong voice for respite in all forums.

American Academy of Pediatrics
National Headquarters
141 Northwest Point Boulevard
P.O. Box 927
Elk Grove Village, Illinois 60007-1098
Phone: (202) 347-8600
Phone: (847) 434-4000
Email: kidsdocs@aap.org

Acknowledgements

I owe a debt of gratitude to both my parents for raising me with the love every child deserves. For each person who encouraged me to write this story, thank you for believing I could. For those who believe this book can make a difference, I hope that is true. For the ones who lived this life, you deserve so much more. Never give up hope.

True
Talent

The First Mistake

T.R. Earnhart

Cassandra Scherer

The
Stone Doorway